A WORLD-CLASS ARAB ASSASSIN named Rashid Haman has reportedly sneaked inside the good ol' U.S. of A. to train a band of in-house American terrorists. "Perfect," Slayton tells himself. "That's all we need—another bunch of bomb-throwing half-wits, too lazy to stand in the employment line."

Then, he hears a new rumor. The maniac's mission is to eliminate the President with deliberate speed.

BEN SLAYTON, T-Man, isn't making cracks anymore. This is serious business, the kind of scheme he knows how to fight.

Books by Buck Sanders

BEN SLAYTON: T-MAN #1
A CLEAR AND PRESENT DANGER

BEN SLAYTON: T-MAN #2
STAR OF EGYPT

Published by
WARNER BOOKS

BEN SLAYTON T-MAN

#2

Star of Egypt

Buck Sanders

WARNER BOOKS

A Warner Communications Company

WARNER BOOKS EDITION

Warner Books, Inc., 75 Rockefeller Plaza, New York, N.Y. 10019

A Warner Communications Company

Printed in the United States of America

First Printing: October, 1981

10 9 8 7 6 5 4 3 2 1

BEN SLAYTON
T-MAN

#2

Star of Egypt

1

The Washington, D.C. police cruiser made the '52 Nash-Healy as it slewed out of the solid rope of traffic jamming the inbound artery. In fact, the sportster had jockeyed to the right in an astounding display of gear-shifting and pilot timing, and was zipping along the breakdown lane pretty as you please when the police flashbar came to life and the cop behind the wheel tore out in pursuit.

"Goddam Georgetown hoity-toities," snarled Officer Max Michaels. He held his own wheel in a death grip, and was itching to use up some of his accumulated offensive-driving repertoire. "Money always thinks it's immune to the law."

"Take a look at her, though," said his partner for the shift, Officer Bran Craddock. "That baby is in A-1 condition." The chrome on the Nash-Healy winked brightly back at them as they gained. The driver could now see the police car in his rearview mirror, yet paid it absolutely no attention.

"Asshole keeps driving it that way, it ain't gonna be in any kind of shape for long," said Michaels.

Craddock ignored his partner, tending instead to business. "I need wants and warrants on Virginia license Victor—Xray—Charlie three-three-six." He waited through the police-band static as, to their left, the cars on the highway crawled along at ten per. They blurred past as though parked.

The cruiser ate up the remaining slack between it and the speeding automobile. "Get on the horn and tell the idiot to pull it over and full stop," said Michaels. "Shit."

Craddock had lifted the mike to his lips when the driver of

the Nash-Healy acknowledged their presence by looking at his mirror and waving his right hand. "What the hell—?"

And then it was gone.

The cruiser careened past the gap in the traffic, and Michaels, cursing, laid on the brakes. A Continental with an overheated radiator had choked off the center lane, while on the right a tow truck had inched up about a car-length and a half. Amazingly, the Nash-Healy had ducked into the gap and slashed across the open space into the far lane without even dropping speed. The police car came to a halt in a fishtailing slide of gravel, stranded on the shoulder.

"Son of a bitch!" shouted Michaels, slamming on the wheel and instantly jacking the vehicle into reverse. Craddock's mouth was hanging open, and he still held the mike. "Get on that thing," yelled Michaels. "Have him cut off at the junction!"

The right-lane gap had closed up with the slow inexorability of a glob of gunk in a lava lamp. The two officers were trapped in the breakdown lane, for ahead of them sprawled a Winnebago with two flat tires. Michaels, sweating, florid, unleashed a chain of profanity that caused two elderly women in a Volkswagen directly across from them to roll up their windows in indignation.

"Beautiful car, though," mused Craddock.

Five minutes later the cruiser, chipping out slow progress on the artery that a few miles back turned into Highway One, was informed that its APB on a 1952 two-seater Nash-Healy sports car, license number VXC-336, had been cancelled, orders-from-headquarters style, and Michaels exploded again.

Benjamin Justin Slayton angled into his private parking slot with nostalgia. He knew he was late—he was practically always late, or as Ham Winship would put it in his ineluctable fashion, "habitually, pathologically, terminally, and irrevocably late." Exclamation point.

But the nostalgia concerned Slayton's brief days on the stock car circuit. It was the thrill of driving fast, the sheer *acceleration,* in all senses, that had kept him from giving in to the logical need to stop and explain to the police that his schedule had priority over a simple traffic jam. A flash of the

ID cards, a quick clearance, and the mad dash toward Washington would have been sanctioned.

That was too much like playing it safe. No dare.

The Nash-Healy was a finely tuned extension of his body. He had cut his driving teeth on the competitive stock tracks, where everything was allowed and structural integrity counted for as much as driving skill and sheer reckless guts. He floored the Nash in the breakdown lane, and for a second, was back on the stock rink, pushing for the winner's circle clearance.

It was during this freewheeling period in his life he had met Jean Marie. After that, the memories became painful.

Now there was Washington, and a change of skins. Now meant shedding the grubby Levi's, leaving his latest half-rebuilt engine—this one, the powerhouse from a 1912 Caddy—behind on the Mount Vernon farm, and losing a five-day growth of beard.

Now, suited, shaven, at a glance no different from the many well-cut denizens of D.C., Ben Slayton was geared for Treasury Department business. It had taken a single name, uttered by his immediate superior, Hamilton Winship (a name that by itself usually provoked a thoughtful pause among the Georgetown gentry), to bring him driving up from Virginia in a singularly humorless state of mind. The slot-car race with the local heat had been a distraction, nothing more.

Now Ben Slayton was thinking in terms of his chances for killing. He was not eccentric, or sadistic, or mad, for that matter. He recognized, with a chilling kind of pragmatism, that in the course of Treasury Department affairs one often runs afoul of individuals a cut above the norm in wiliness and extralegal aspirations—and frequently those individuals might try to kill a government employee who might be less alert, less aware.

This could easily be discounted as paranoia, he thought, as he gathered up his coat and briefcase. But the special division founded in the Treasury Department by Winship a few years previously had been established with a keen eye toward that which was usually dismissed as "cuckoo conspiracy theories." In a sense, a kind of paranoia—paranoia realized—was essential to their work in this suborganization.

The Irish Republican Army dealt in paranoia. The Mau-

Mau dealt in paranoia. Black September, ditto. All were the worst type of urban terrorists; all dealt professionally in death.

Slayton was pragmatic. Like it or not, urban terrorism had come to America as well, and as he himself had put it months before, "America had damned well be ready to deal with it, just as professionally."

He was alone in the shadows of the subsurface garage. The name that Winship had primed him with also meant paranoia, and death. Slayton felt the peculiar, humming tension zipping along his muscles, tightening up his frame. It was the same way before each new assignment. He jammed his coded card into the elevator slot: the access bar blinked green, and the steel doors slid smoothly open.

In five brisk minutes he had run the upstairs security gauntlet. In two more he found himself staring across a vast expanse of lacquered oak desk at his superior, Hamilton Winship. Winship's direct, administrative gray eyes, under their slightly bushy white brows, met Slayton's brown ones.

He dropped the dossier folder he had been examining on the desk top, and it made a loud *smack* in the utter silence of the room.

"What do you know about Egyptology?"

"Good morning, sir," Slayton said, at roughly the same time Winship spoke. Winship neither flinched, nor blinked, remaining immobile behind the desk.

After a beat Slayton picked up the ball and sprinted. "Well, sir, I know the difference between Horus and Anubis and Amen-Ra. I know Horus was the son of Isis, and Osirus; that Isis was, among other things, Osiris' sister. Seth was something of a pain." He paused, but did not fritter. "I was a big fan of the Mummy when I was a kid."

Methodically, Winship revolved the dossier and slid it across the desk top, toward Slayton. "Become as intimate with that as you can," he said. "God knows I've tried."

"To what end, sir?" Slayton was still standing with his hands clasped behind his back. The heavy, stilted atmosphere of Winship's lair, exactly like an old British gentleman's club, always managed to put Slayton just a touch ill at ease. The furniture was mostly overstuffed red leather; the accoutrements included the usual framed photos of Winship posing with every President since Truman; and the air forever carried the faint tang of rough-cut pipe tobacco. Winship always went for his pipe when blueprinting strategies, and he fished it out of a punchbowl-sized ashtray now.

"In two days an American ship of Egyptian registry—the *Star of Egypt,* in fact—will dock in Baltimore. It will be loaded down with artifacts from the pyramids, notably items from the recent digs at Giza and new finds from the Seth-Olet tombs uncovered last year." He fired up the pipe and the air was immediately clouded in dense webs of smoke.

"This will be structured very much like the King Tut tour," he continued, "save that the debut is being reserved for Washington, a high-level kickoff at which the President will officiate, opening the show to the United States, so to speak. The overseers of the tour are a pack of principally British scientists and archeological types, plus Egyptian and Arab workers. The company bulks out at twenty or so people."

His eyes moved up to meet Slayton's again. "We have reason to suspect that one of these people is Rashid Haman." It was the name that had brought Slayton up from Mount Vernon.

Slayton picked up the dossier.

"There'll be quite a lot of speechmaking and lip-service to cultural exchange, that sort of thing. . . ."

"All of which is road-smoothing for more armament deals and other juicy items the American public isn't as interested in as Egyptian artifacts," Slayton concluded. "It figures."

"There are détente angles, petroleum angles, and, politically speaking, the whole thing could be loaded with gunpowder, if Haman really is part of the entourage."

"A bunch of priceless and irreplaceable artifacts," mused Slayton. "If anything was to get scratched, the whole country loses face. The President knows, of course, he may be stepping into a pair of cross-hairs if Haman is around?"

"Yes. Strict security precautions are mandatory. The CIA is handling some of the particulars."

"The CIA is also the bunch that botched the trap for Haman in 1974," said Slayton. "Is the photo in here?" He indicated the dossier, and Winship nodded, almost imperceptibly.

Slayton riffled through it and found a glossy blowup, the only photograph the entire covert resources of the United

States had been able to produce of Rashid Haman. It was black and white, incredibly grainy, and, to Slayton, obviously taken by a tyro who did not know enough about telephoto lenses. Shown turning in profile was a man of medium height, heavily bearded, wearing dark wrap-around sunglasses. Totally useless. Even money the beard was fake; two-to-one odds that Haman was aware of the photographer at the time. Haman was dangerously good.

"Shit," he breathed.

"I'm aware of the limitations of our sister services," said Winship, knocking out the bowl of his pipe. "That is why you are here."

"This whole mess is a setup, ripe for a symbolic coup of some sort," said Slayton. "You know that, surely. So does the President. It's so obvious, especially given the factor of Haman."

"What other reasons would Haman have for coming to America?" said Winship.

Slayton shuffled absently through the remainder of the folder. "The only reason I can come up with that holds water isn't very nice. Haman did a gig for the I.R.A. once; and certainly his concerns are global. He's about as devout a Sunni Moslem as the Pope. He needs a lot of capital to grease the escape wheels for his extranational operations. Enough money will send him anywhere—he'd probably kill *himself* if there was enough *baksheesh* in it." He dropped the folder on the desk, more as punctuation than anything. "If he's not here to go after the President, then he's here as a teacher. He could train a cadre of urban terrorists that would make the CIA look like college sophomores jerking off."

Winship nodded professorially.

"The tour is as good a cover as any; we know he could move into the country undetected if he wanted to. If he's not with the tour, the rumor that he is is a diversion, most likely initiated by Haman himself. Same trick as the Black September operation in '77, when everyone heard he was in France. Everybody believed it long enough for him to hit a Japanese industrialist in broad daylight in Yokohama. He was supposed to be in Canada during that mess with the Iranian Embassy."

"Thus, the importance of investigating," said Winship, letting Slayton sew the skein of events together for himself.

"We have to know whether he's really here or not. Either way, it's an ominous development. Whenever that guy moves, the ears of his enemies prick up. That's about half the people in the civilized world. Implanting the information that he is smuggling himself into America via the tour would be a perfect way to draw attention away from the tour itself." With a bitter little grin Slayton added, "Thus do the wheels of international intrigue grind and grind."

Winship shifted himself back to business. "For the moment, you greet the members of the tour, acting as an American liason, a sort of high-priced tour guide."

"Right. All smiles and urbane charm." Slayton's eyes darkened. "And if I make Haman. . . ?"

"You're a free agent," Winship said. "Act as the conditions dictate."

Slayton scooped up the dossier, already thinking that the first order of business was elementary research. He headed for the office door. As he was on his way out, Winship harrumphed loudly, an almost petulant expression on his face.

"Sir?"

"Be discreet," Winship said, somewhat plaintively.

Slayton smiled. "I always am, sir." His exit was smooth.

Benjamin Slayton wanted very much to kill Rashid Haman.

2

The Capitol Building dome glowed, huge and golden. With the darkness of night to obscure the litter and the other less photogenic aspects of the nation's capital, Washington, D.C. looked just like a picture postcard. The air was heavy with moisture.

Around Ben Slayton, the traffic strobed into abstract blurs of red and yellow light. He was thinking about a man named Barney Kaufman.

Elfin-faced, bright-eyed, with a perpetual grin that could light up a room, Barney Kaufman had been the man who introduced Slayton to what he termed "the sleazy delights of Tangier." Slayton had been through Morocco only once before in his life, a fly-by through the capital city of Rabat that did not really count as a visit, and so had taken up Barney's jovial offer of an interesting place to dispense with some accumulated leave-time back in November of 1978.

Barney Kaufman was an ex-CIA agent. International applications and troubleshooting. Barney Kaufman, jovial, smiling Barney, had killed maybe fifty people in his lifetime, one at a time, with garrotes, karate, point-blank dum-dum shells, long-range sniping, broken beer bottles, and arranged accidents. Once he described to Slayton how he had killed a man by punching a ballpoint pen into his brain through the eye socket.

Slayton, in turn, described some of his chores as a fighter-bomber pilot in Vietnam. To Slayton, there was little moral distinction to be made between breaking some Polish double agent's back with your knee and blowing Viet Cong to bits, flaming entire tracts of land and sending people running and screaming with their hair on fire. Kaufman had retired from the CIA. Slayton left Nam and was honorably discharged.

There was an easy camaraderie between the two men. Both were passionate about personal ethics, not causes. They made no apologies to each other. It looked as though they might spend some good times together, raising hell in foreign countries and generally making a happy shambles of the clichéed images of Americans abroad.

Ben Slayton was sitting three feet away from Barney Kaufman when Rashid Haman's guerrillas hit the Tangier cabaret in which they were dining.

"This *bouillabaisse* will curl your hair, buddy," Barney had said. "Sort of like the food you get at the McDonald's in Paris."

"Subtly unlike the domestic stuff, I gather?" Slayton grinned over his glass and nodded in somber approbation of the nearly naked and astoundingly brown dancer quivering not five feet away. The band was loud and raucous, but their instruments were ancient. Slayton appreciated Barney's taste.

"Well, French hamburgers are made from beef that's grass-fed, not corn-fed. If you're not prepared for the taste—" He grimaced. "Phew! And they make milkshakes out of water."

"They don't even use milk in them in America anymore, so what's the difference?"

At that moment the frenzy of the dancer's gyrations caused her magnificent breasts to burst free of her costume. They were finely toned—the dancing muscles helped—and exhibited deep brown buds. She merely smiled at her audience, showing fine white teeth and a dark, gypsylike face, and continued dancing.

"To stop the dance in the middle of the story would be a *faux pas* of major proportions," shouted Barney, rapping knuckles on the rough-hewn table in time to the music. The woman returned Slayton's appreciative smile enthusiastically. She had the darkest eyes Slayton had ever seen.

"Why are we sitting here talking about hamburgers and milkshakes?" he yelled back over the din, and both men broke up laughing.

Barney had raised his glass in the general direction of both Slayton and the dancer, when the top of his head was torn off by a salvo of 9-millimeter slugs from a Smith and Wesson M76 submachine gun in the grip of a man in a black fighting suit standing in the small entrance foyer to the cabaret. More men crowded in behind him, weapons bristling. A thermite jug went noisily off behind the bar, cutting what little electricity illuminated the place, and everything was plunged into panic and blackness.

Slayton hit the deck, tearing a Baretta Brigadier he had borrowed from Barney away from the shoulder holster he wore. His shirtfront was spattered with his friend's blood and brains, and he could feel viscous moisture speckling his face as well. It took only a second for his eyes to adjust to the ambient candlelight in the large room. He snapped off two clean rounds, and saw a silhouette near the entrance jerk backward and drop in a sprawl. Slayton was up and moving before anyone could fix his position.

The dark room was alive with screams and shouts, shooting, and rampant movement. Slayton body-rolled across an open space, coming to a crouch and up-ending a filled table into the path of a guerrilla nearly invisible in his black outfit. The man pivoted into a forearm smash from Slayton that cleaned his feet from under him. His head cracked on the table edge, and Slayton drove the heel of his hand into the man's throat, crushing his larynx. He did not get up.

Slayton snatched up his weapon, an Uzi submachine gun his hands recognized even in the dark, and sprayed the doorway in two arcs. He fixed on return fire, and cut down a man holding a pistol near the flaming remnants of the bar.

Like that, it was over. Apparently the guerrillas had hit their mark and fled, taking less than forty-five seconds for the entire operation.

Maybe their mark had been Barney, Slayton thought uneasily. It was not unlikely. All men like himself had enemies; sometimes it did come to this. And if he had been sitting about a foot to the left, he would be on the floor with his friend, fodder for the morgue, instead of picking the ID and personals off his corpse.

Slayton took Barney's belongings, and in so doing took

responsibility for his friend until they put him in the ground. He told the relatives and those who needed to be told. He dispatched his primary obligation of honor.

Two days after the fracas, Slayton learned through Interpol that the hit had been arranged through Egyptian shipping interests, using imported thugs. The dead bodies in black suits, two of whom Slayton had killed, would never be traced. They were picked to be linked to Palestinian interests if killed. A lot of Moroccan cash, laundered via Saudi Arabia, had paid for the hit. The targets turned out to be a table-load of minor-league Egyptian shipping executives who happened to be sitting several yards away from Slayton and Barney. It was specified that the hit be messy, and leave a lot of bodies. It was, and it did.

Slayton also learned that the hit was used by the Black September terrorist named Rashid Haman as a dry run for a more important assassination assignment, to follow several weeks later in Johannesburg. Barney had been murdered purely as local color for Rashid Haman.

As he drove, the Washington weather now threatening rain, he thought of Barney, dumped unceremoniously on the cabaret floor in a welter of black blood, and of the topless cabaret dancer, flung over a broken chair like a dirty shirt, her left foot jutting upward in the stillness of death, her fine, fine body perforated by at least ten Uzi bullets.

As a special troubleshooter for Treasury, Slayton sometimes acted as a contra-terrorist, who employed the same moves and methods as men like Haman. He was not a government hit man. He knew himself to be different in an important, basic, chemical way. But thinking now about Barney and Rashid Haman, he was damned if he could name that precise difference to himself at the moment.

"I had a premonition I might find you moping around here. This makes three times in recent memory you've bounced back to Washington without calling me."

Slayton looked up from his mostly untouched *medallions de veau au bec rouge* with *sauce milo* and instantly felt a sting of sheepishness. Yes, he should have called. Wilma Christian was worth a call, despite his packed and mechanically tedious day.

He had spent most of his time poring over a Treasury Department security A-priority computer terminal, extracting information to construct a rise-and-fall graph of Rashid Haman's terrorist activity. Slayton preferred having vital details centralized into his own handwritten notations on a yellow legal pad—often, his own constructs yielded patterns the machines and the political experts overlooked. One by-product of his labor was adrenalin; it accumulated poisonously in his system as he documented Haman's activities into boxes subgrouped by *real, suspected,* and *advisory* participations. He could not cleanse Barney Kaufman's face from his mind, and the negative energy he had dammed up toward the faceless entity known as Rashid Haman proved to be frustrating. Slayton felt a surge of relief—or something like it—upon looking up and recognizing a friendly face.

"I could blame dereliction of duty, but I don't think you'd buy it," he offered. "How about preoccupation? No?"

Wilma smiled. Slayton had already risen at the approach of the waiter who threaded Wilma back toward the private, three-quarter carrel where he dined, and now Wilma slid easily in beside him.

"You look like you're starving," he said.

"Jesus, Ben, a line like that I thought you'd reserve for the high-schoolers you like to molest," she said with a light smirk. Looking toward his plate, she added, "I might order something later, maybe. After I do this." And she leaned over and planted a delicious, welcome-home kiss on his lips.

Slayton forgot about the fair-to-middling French concoction before him.

Access to A-priority terminals had all sorts of advantages. For example, according to the machine records, *CHRISTIAN, WILMA B(LAIR), b. 06/13/50 ss# 527-55-1937,* was a *WFA,* had *bl/br,* was *5'9¾"* and *130lb* and was cross-indexed under *JOURNALISTS,* among other categories that somehow related to her professions, her upbringing, likes, dislikes, or political leanings/potentials.

"Hello," she said, breaking the kiss at last.

Slayton cleared his throat. "Evening, ma'am."

What Wilma Christian actually was was a soft and incredibly wily creature in a field whose beat, the nation's capital, often required uncompromisingly dirty play from those who tried to succeed as reporters and journalists. Her fabulous cascade of hair was a mellow sandalwood color, not brown, and her eyes a brilliant Danish blue, the irises ringed in direct black—eyes that commanded attention. She was a hard-core professional whose beauty frequently butted opponents off-kilter, and one way or another she ran whatever she needed to earth, in due course. She was perhaps one of the five top reporters in the city.

And sometimes, Slayton added mentally, she had just a little trouble reconciling her ethics with her news sense. But then everyone did . . . even Treasury agents.

He was a bit perturbed by the immediate way she asked him the question he knew was coming: "You on assignment?"

He let it off lightly. "Of course. And no, it's not open for discussion. Next topic. Cheers." He raised his glass as the waiter returned with Wilma's martini.

"Sorry," she said. "Mata Hari strikes again. One of us will learn. So anyway, why has my phone not been alive with invitations to visit you in Virginia again?"

"You're the only houseguest I've ever had that didn't wait for a butler to putter in to clean up after her, did you know that?" Of course she did.

"Evasive, Slayton. Good god." A pause. "Your august presence in Washington doesn't have anything to do with the President's crowing about 'more visible political figures,' does it?"

Slayton frowned into his wine.

"Okay, okay, change of tack," she said. "Wherever you dumped your attache case, let's stop there and get whatever you may need on the way back to my flat."

"Actually, I've been sleeping with my pet computer console," said Slayton.

"Isn't the pillow talk a bit, um, stilted?"

"Practically prefabricated."

"One more, and this one isn't so much nosy as personal interest: when do you have to go to work?"

"Sunday morning," he said, too quickly.

"Ah. That afternoon I'm off anyway. Some British embassy types are uncrating a tomb-load of Egyptian incunabula up in Maryland, and I have to cover it."

Slayton's expression remained comfortably neutral. It had

happened before—pure coincidence. Even if Wilma spotted him around, she knew enough not to draw attention to him.

She was past the future assignment already, and onto items of more personal import. "Well, sir, the weekend fairly glitters before us."

He deliberately tried to sound cowed. "Gee, Wilma, I should have called, I mean, gosh, I . . ."

"Oh, shut up," she said as he finished off his wine. "Mom and Dad won't mind, and besides—"

Slayton's eyes grew very white as he almost spluttered. "Mom and Dad. . . ?" he rasped.

She reached over to him. "Just kidding, just kidding. You high-power government types take everything so goddam *seriously*." Now she could not keep from smiling. Slayton laughed out loud.

He hated to admit it, but Wilma was just the person he needed to keep Barney Kaufman's ghost from prodding him, to put the black flood-tide of hatred for Rashid Haman on hold so it did not shred away his gut. With anyone else that evening, he might have become vindictive, preoccupied. He lucked out; Wilma had found him.

Her smile was a distinctive and enriching thing. It still adorned her face as he tossed his junk onto the marble-topped table in the cramped little foyer to her apartment. She came sprinting out of the kitchen before he even got the door closed, and leapt into his arms, guiding his hands beneath her ski sweater, eagerly molding her mouth over his.

"I've got a jug of very cold Rhine in the fridge," she managed, between breaths.

"Somehow I'm not very thirsty right now." She held up her arms, and he pulled the sweater up from the bottom, remembering her admonishments to *be gentle to the material, damn it.*

In a sort of mad party tangle of limbs, they helped to divest each other of clothing while running an equally mad line of chitchat that seemingly had very little to do with sex.

"I see you got the window fixed."

"You know how mad a drafty hairline crack can make you when you sleep with the heat off? *Jesus!*"

"How come you get so much junk mail?"

"Nice tie. A he-present or a she-present?"

"I haven't gotten around to underwear monogrammed by the days of the week yet, but I manage."

"Hey, the carpet's new, too. Feel the shag; it's very nice . . ."

"Don't forget about the heat—" They both stopped. Her eyes shone blackly in the darkness, and he said, "It's very nice to be with you again. And I promise I'll call. Next time." He smiled disarmingly.

"Liar. My mother warned me about your type, liar!" She pushed him, and they both wound up on the floor, naked and laughing. They eventually made it to the Rhine jug in the refrigerator. In between, the carpet was luxurious, and clean-smelling, and very, very nice.

3

The *Star of Egypt* was a relic of the middle-1950s shipping boom, constructed before the United States ever fretted about OPEC or worried about hydrogenization lobbies. Even before he saw the ship, Slayton spotted the red, white, and black bands of the Egyptian flag above the third-story roofs of a cluster of corrugated-steel dock storage areas.

There was a nickel-plated .45 automatic in the glove compartment of Slayton's inconspicuous Triumph. The hammer was down on an empty chamber, and the car was locked. There was no reason to pack heat during his initial tour of the ship and docking facilities.

The *Star of Egypt* dominated the scene, extending back seemingly to the horizon. Give her two or three more years, thought Slayton, and she'll be signed over to commercial petroleum service like all the rest—but right now she was pretty impressive.

Slayton saw the first guard instantly, and starting from there it was simple to pinpoint the others. Security people always milled around in a pattern, however unconscious, and if you could nail one, it was easy to project the locations of his buddies. These men, Slayton knew, were bona fide guards from the Sparta Security Agency Ltd. He had often seen Brinks and Pinkerton dregs that appeared to walk off-kilter when strapped to a weapon; the Sparta men were for the most part ex-military or ex-specialist, and they knew what gunplay was all about, should shooting become necessary. It appeared fairly obvious that neither the Cairo Museum, the

British Museum, nor the specialists in attendance during the tour were taking any chances.

The nearest sentry was already glaring at him, prepared to impede his progress if he tried to venture inside the cordon of sawhorses and yellow rope that sectioned off the unloading area. He pulled the credentials brief from inside his suit. He was legitimate.

The guard, whose tag read *Stackman*, was already into his spiel as Slayton handed him the brief: "I'm sorry, sir, but access to this area is prohibited." He was shifting his balance —an authority gesture, thought Slayton disconnectedly—as his eyes ran down the credentials. He straightened almost self-consciously, then spoke with an air of camaraderie. "You're Rademacher. Excuse me, sir." He snapped the brief shut and handed it back. Slayton nodded.

"Where do I find Willis?" he said.

"On board, I think, sir."

"Who is your crew chief?"

"Frank Groth. Standing over by the ramp, there."

"Thank you, Mr. Stackman." Slayton wheeled and walked briskly toward the ramp with just a tinge of self-satisfaction. It did not look as if he were going to have any trouble.

"Yes, sir," Stackman said to Slayton's back, mentally cursing command hierarchies.

Slayton spotted a man who had to be Professor Gordon Willis. He was standing on the loading ramp, towering over Frank Groth in a wobbly way, belaboring something terribly important. The spiked brown beard and the spectacles fit Slayton's preconception of the man. Hanging a little too loosely on his tail and bony frame, Willis' suit fluttered against the light breeze. He was waving his arms like a symphony conductor.

"*Because* these men, while somewhat lacking in other areas, *know their jobs* in this one, Mr. Groth! If they were not so slow, as you say, we might have a disaster. Those cases?" He pointed and Groth turned. "Hermetically sealed. They contain a gas for the preservation of the artifacts; that gas is odorless as well as colorless. Thus, if we rupture a case in unloading, we may not know the gas has escaped until it is too late. So I think, Mr. Groth, that a certain amount of care—which you might interpret as laziness or slowness on the part of my workers—is justified in this case!" Without so much as a beat, Willis spun his head and zeroed in on Slayton. "Yes?"

Slayton extended his hand. "Ben Rademacher, Mr. Willis. I'm here to—"

"Professor," said Willis, icily.

"Professor Willis, sorry." Slayton smiled diplomatically. "Here to oversee—"

"My security, yes, I know. I was *informed,"* he clarified, "by phone calls and letters and documentation—and does your government *really* waste all that paper to make sure of what it is doing? Hm." He shook Slayton's hand. "At any rate, I'm pleased to deal with you, mister . . . um, Rademacher, yes." He was already ignoring Groth.

"If it's not too much of an imposition, Professor," said Slayton, picking up a cue from the cooling argument between the two other men, "I'd like to meet the other principal members of the tour as soon as it's convenient."

Groth interposed himself, sticking out his hand. "Groth, Mr. Rademacher."

Slayton disposed of the duty. "Right, Mr. Groth. I'll speak to you as soon as I get oriented here."

Willis, who was preoccupied with brushing imaginary lint from his coat, muttered, "That will be all for now." Groth made a gruff noise and loped off, the gear on his belt clanking. Willis watched him go.

"Well," he said, looking up. "My contingent." He turned to indicate the *Star of Egypt,* as huge as a skyscraper on its side, extending in all directions behind him. "Should be easy enough to locate them; they're *in there* somewhere. God knows they're not hefting these crates around or doing anything that remotely relates to our schedule. But please, sir, don't get me wrong—they're invaluable, all of them." Willis' sentences flowed into one another in a tailgating fashion, with no gaps left for Slayton to jump into, like a running one-man monologue that regarded an audience as only a matter of convenience. Willis had already turned and his long, spindly legs were taking him up the steeply canted ramp with more assurance than was apparent when he said—not bothering to speak to Slayton, since he had turned—"Follow me, we'll go seek them out. Rather like mucking about in a tomb, looking for secret doors. Ah, well."

Obediently, Slayton kept pace, already oddly fond of the rambling professor before him. There was no doubt that he, at least, was bona fide. Slayton's quick reading of the professor's personal history had left him impressed. In his heyday, Professor Gordon Willis had been one to slog down into filthy hovels and dig with bare hands, uncovering finds and artifacts that the armchair Egyptologists who made their dole from quarterly journals had speculated could not possibly exist. Willis went in and proved them wrong, betraying a maverick spirit Slayton found easy to relate to. Slayton liked dealing with men who knew what they were talking about. And he could generally smell an imposter, thanks to senses honed by dealing with professionals—everyone from professional Washington power brokers to professional Harlem knife-fighters, from sophisticated international secret agents to street-corner whores.

He turned back into Willis' running line of patter.

"Of course, this warehouse business only increases risk, if you ask me, because it just adds one more time everything must be moved; one more time we might make an error." He seemed to catch himself, smiling. "But of course, if *we* don't know what we're doing, why are we here at all?"

Why indeed. Slayton's problem was that although all the characters present were, in fact, professionals, one of them might be a professional of a deadlier sort.

"Of course, I don't pretend that the government involvement in all of this"—he spread his hands expansively—"indicates the slightest interest in the artifacts themselves. It's all politics, all greasing up the right palms, and showing the correct face to the world at large. Everyone else is always watching, eager to pass judgment. So we put on our little burlesques." He glanced back at Slayton. "This *is* a singular discovery, you know," he said, his eyes now glinting with the prospect of discussing his specialty. "Do you, sir, have the slightest interest in all of this?"

Slayton was prepared for a question like that one, and his reply was calculated as well. "I don't know everything about the Seth-Olet discovery that I should, Professor, but I do understand that it wasn't your traditional pyramid."

"In fact," Willis said, pointing the way down a narrow corridor, and indicating a potential head bump for Slayton to avoid, "the Seth-Olet tomb was more properly a *mastăba.* One of the reasons the more cursory explorers missed it—they were locked into the idea that they would find Seth-Olet inside a normal pyramid."

"Oh," began Slayton, delivering his punchline: "So the fact that you found a *mastăba* means that not only did your predecessors have the wrong shape, but the wrong dating, as well. Generally, *mastăbas* predate the pyramids, don't they? And even if they didn't, you'd be able to place the body in proper historical perspective merely by the methods used to mummify it, once you'd found it."

Willis stopped, and, in the semidarkness of the corridor, Slayton nearly collided with him. He turned slowly, almost theatrically, and fixed Slayton with a cocked eye. "Yes." Then, almost conspiratorially, "Follow me and I'll unveil some of Seth-Olet's secrets for you." He left off *if you're interested,* and Ben Slayton considered his second acid test of the day passed.

4

The dark-haired woman assessed herself in the narrow cabin mirror. She shifted weight to one leg and cocked the other, watching the light catch and slip along the fine leather of her boots. Not too thick or clunky, she thought; it would be easy to be graceful in these. The light skirt she had chosen hid her well-molded legs, but was less a restriction of style than a concession to appearing the proper academic when stepping off the ship. And it looked good.

From the waist up she was naked, and she turned, inspecting the way her stance affected the play of her breasts.

"Egomaniac," came a sarcastic voice through the connecting cabin door.

The woman before the mirror shook her head, whipping the fluffy black hair around. "Just like an American commercial, right?" she said into the mirror.

Into the cabin leaned another woman, wearing a conservative pantsuit and expensive, but understated, jewelry. Her hair was a framing spill of tight tan curls; she looked more naturally the academic type. "Shauna," she said, with sisterly good humor, "there will be television cameras."

"Do you think they'd go for this?" said Shauna, deliberately squeezing in her shoulders and moving in a sinuous little dance before the glass.

"Might be a grabber to open the tour," the woman shrugged. "What you would call a narrative hook."

There was an impatient knocking on the outside cabin door. "I'll get it," said the other woman under her breath, as Shauna snatched up a safari blouse and quickly buttoned herself into it.

Professor Willis bustled into the cabin as the door opened, already in the midst of his presentation, as usual. "Well, thank god you two are where you're supposed to be, anyway . . . um, Doctors, may I present to you—you can come in, Mr. Rademacher, no need to stand on ceremony in the bowels of this hulking ship, for heaven's sake!"

Slayton, standing on the threshold, stepped in, nodding at the two women.

"As I was saying, Doctors, may I present Mr. Benjamin Rademacher. He will oversee our security while in Washington, including the loading, unloading, the trucking of the artifacts to the capital, and so on. He is also here in the unofficial capacity of troubleshooter, complaint department, and so forth." The four were now faced off.

"Mr. Rademacher, this is Dr. Margaret Leiber."

The woman in the pantsuit smiled and extended a hand that was cool and dry. "Maggie," she said. She had the large, rounded lower lip that is one of the hallmarks of British beauty.

"And this is Dr. Shauna Ramsey."

Her eyes were dark and inviting, reminding Slayton instantly of the dancer in Tangier. Her eyes were evaluating him up and down quite frankly. One hand lingered near the open throat of the safari shirt, as though she regretted buttoning so far up. Her other hand squeezed his lightly while she continued to stare into his eyes.

"I don't know of your specific fields, ladies," said Slayton, "but I do know a bit about Professor Willis' work, and admire you in advance as part of his team. It is a pleasure to meet you both." He managed to dredge up the Ben Slayton-charmer-smile, and both women reciprocated warmly.

Slayton registered vibrations of easy caution. Nothing, however, set his internal danger mechanisms off. A vague disquiet, that was all.

"Thank god," said Shauna, displaying a British lilt equal to Maggie's, a tonal quality of voice that could soften iron. "We did so think they would saddle us with a dreary academic, or an intellectual eunuch. You're not a dreary academic, are you, Mr. Rademacher?" Her eyes were already broadcasting a separate message on another frequency.

"Nor a eunuch of any variety, Ms. Ramsey," he said. It was apparently the correct response.

"Gordie, when can we get out of here and get to the hotel? My body is prepared for American facilities, if not for American food," said Maggie.

Willis shrugged again. "You two aren't especially needed here now. Ahmed and the crew will be here tonight, along with the security people. It will take that long, and probably most of tomorrow, just to unload in the proper fashion. I'm sure you could breeze over to the hotel now."

"Does this mean you must loiter around the dock until dawn, Mr. Rademacher, just to insure the safety of Egypt's heritage?" Shauna tilted her head down as she spoke, fixing him still with her enigmatic eyes.

"No, fortunately, Ms. Ramsey," said Slayton. "I am a security representative, not a security guard. My stock in trade is being five places at once and getting the impossible done on time and under budget, if you know what I mean."

"How lucky for us," murmured Willis, "considering that incompetent Groth, out there."

"He's beefing about the hours, mainly, Professor. His boys are up to it if he's not. Let me worry about him, too."

Willis sighed, as though done with the matter. "A relief, to be sure. Shall we continue the tour?"

He nodded to himself, "Yes." To the women, he added, "I hope we'll have time to dine and talk later, but now those damnable obligations of duty must hold sway. Being British—"

"We understand such obligations too well!" laughed Maggie. "Forever the victims of stereotyping, I suppose."

"After you, Professor," Slayton offered. "Until later, then, ladies," he added. The cabin door swung shut with a solid *thunk*.

"Ciao," said Maggie.

"Good evening," said Shauna.

Both women turned and regarded each other, pointedly, as soon as the hatch was closed.

The secondary hold on the *Star of Egypt* was a huge and

dank affair, glutted with shapeless cargo, all lashed and crated and padded against the jostling of shipment. The smells were of dust, salt water, light lubricants, canvas, and hemp. Professor Willis led Slayton through the badly lit maze of cargo, wielding a large emergency flashlight.

"All this has yet to be moved to the warehouse," he said. "Then another checklist, another inventory; we take stock almost daily sometimes. Some of the crating material we use is constructed very much like those Oriental boxes-within-boxes-within-boxes. We transport the dead of Egypt in the same fashion the Egyptians themselves used to entomb them, in multiple coffins."

When the two men were alone in the thick of the stacked and labelled incunabula, Willis stopped and shone the light directly in Slayton's face. Slayton's heart jumped, but his body tensed.

"Just who are you, Mr. Rademacher, I mean *really,* and what is your purpose here?" The voice was direct, clinical, and humorless. The change itself was unnerving.

Slayton's business, however, was dealing with unnerving situations, and he didn't miss a beat. "Top level and top secret, Professor. You mentioned the political burlesques that governments are so fond of. I'm here to insure such a thing does not happen. Surely you've guessed that by now." He had his hands out before him in honest entreaty.

The Professor's lamp did not waver, and for all the difference it made, they might have been deep inside the twists and turns of a pyramid in the Nile Valley, Slayton's life in the Professor's hands. "Flattering my intellect is not exactly a direct answer, Mr. Rademacher."

"If any of these relics around us were to be damaged, or destroyed, there would be political reverberations, I'm sure. Professor, the only reason I'm here is to see that that doesn't happen." Slayton did not gild his cover story any further. To become talkative on such short notice would give him away.

Still Willis remained immobile. Finally, he said, "Hm." He turned away and continued leading Slayton through the maze, as though nothing had happened.

By touring the remaining holds in sequence, Slayton was for the first time able to get an estimate of the sheer size of the articles that made up the Seth-Olet tour. There were over a thousand major pieces, and the tour was to differ from the Tutankhamen show in that the setups for Seth-Olet and his burial trappings were to sport local color, that is, the items from the tomb would be presented in a surrogate tomb, the better to present the traditional arrangements of such items to the lay public and simultaneously spice the proceedings a bit, should it look too much like a dusty history lesson. There were some canny PR minds at work on this project, as well as eccentric scientists, beautiful women, and a lone terrorist or two.

Slayton heaved an exasperated breath. Sometimes he preferred the straightforward honesty of a fight in a darkened alley, with broken bottles or whatever was handy.

The sensation of emerging from the depths of the *Star of Egypt* was also unsettling, as it was already long past dusk. The wind had turned the lowering temperature into a formidable chill factor, and whipped at the men's clothing as they came back up on deck. Below, the Arab workers and the Sparta men hunched against the wind in heavy coats. The cordoned area was now ringed in yellow service lights. Near the main door of the warehouse one man had a hot plate and a coffeepot going. Slayton was made aware of the insufficiency of his jacket, but Willis did not seem to mind the cold. Considering that his usual stomping ground was the sun-baked Egyptian desert, it seemed unfair.

Willis led Slayton back to the ramp almost automatically, like a butler, but as Slayton started down he reached out and stayed him with a hand on his shoulder.

"Mr. Rademacher, I see no reason whatsoever to tell the others. I will support whatever you say as regards the safety of the exhibits. Might I also add that the presence of someone in your capacity working on this comforts me. Good night to you, sir." He turned briskly and was gone, presumably to settle down with a dense text and a hot toddy.

Slayton could not help grinning to himself. "Good night, Professor."

His check-in with Groth's contingent was a matter of dancing through preset moves, giving directives he knew full well were bullshit, yet required if he were to maintain his façade. Penetrating the whole group, and, to his more immediate end, verifying the presence of Rashid Haman, would take time. Groth's men would dismiss Slayton as FBI or CIA. Slayton gave them a mental once-over and decided that seeking Haman among the guards was stupid. That was that.

Slayton's skin was tingling with the cold by the time he reached the Triumph. His key, however, stopped short of the lock as he bent, eyes suddenly coming into very sharp focus, and concentrated on the juncture of window and roof. Even in the dim light he could make out thin white scratches on the insulating rubber strip.

Slayton moved to the opposite door and, after a quick similar inspection, opened it. At first glance the interior of the car appeared unviolated, but he noticed smudges of dirt on the carpeting, on the side that had held no passengers for weeks. He switched on the interior light.

The driver's side window had been professionally jacked, and only the faint marks on the insulation told the tale. That eliminated burglary; a thief would have jacked-and-snapped the door handle, or just broken the window. Slayton's gaze immediately flew down. There were no tracers or detonation leads attached to the doorwells.

It was the first move in an agonizing touchy process.

He gave the engine what they referred to in the Department as a "British bomb school once-over," and checked out the boot and chassis. Twenty minutes later, satisfied that the Triumph had been entered but not rigged, he popped open the glove compartment. The nickel-plated .45 automatic lay as he had left it, but away from the driver's side door, safety on.

He inspected it in the light. No prints. Then he snapped back the action and a shell popped out. It dropped and lay on the carpeting, its brass gleaming dully.

Whoever had entered the car had done the same thing, evidently unable to tell by mere weight whether or not the gun was loaded. Their inspection had left a slug in a chamber that Slayton had left empty, the slug that had just been ejected.

Slayton pocketed the stray shell and replaced the gun in the glove compartment. There was nothing in the Triumph that would identify who he really was, or compromise him in any way. The car was "document-naked," and the registration and papers would bear out whatever story he cared to spin.

There were personals within, but of a totally nonincriminating nature. The Triumph was clean for Slayton.

Yet someone had checked out his car. The visit had been careful enough that only the most alert would notice the intrusion at all.

Slayton's adrenalin surged. If someone had put a make on him already, they had to be flushed out. And if someone suspected, if they were jumpy enough to boost into his car, perhaps they were jumpy enough to give themselves away. . . .

He slammed the car door a little too hard, and headed back to the unloading area. Stackman was still pulling sentry duty.

The two men nodded at each other, a silent comment on the cold and the unpleasantness of jobs that nevertheless had to be done, and Slayton said, "Any of these Arab or Egyptian workers check out of here tonight, for any reason?"

"No sir. They've been busy right here practically ever since the *Star* docked. I think they're still even sleeping on board. They stick to this area."

"Nobody went out for booze, or anything?"

"No. Their papers are all in order, and of course they're welcome to cruise the city if they like. But it looks like they don't like."

"Double-check?"

"Yes sir. Regardless of their freedom of movement, we're instructed to sign them in or out if they go anywhere." Stackman turned a clipboard up to the light so Slayton could see it: neatly graphed forms. Willis had signed out and returned some twenty times—naturally, as head of the exhibit, he would find himself playing gopher whether he enjoyed it or not. He had also told Slayton that he did not trust the workers as drivers on American roads. The trucking of the artifacts to Washington would be done by domestic drivers.

Shauna Ramsey and Maggie Leiber had signed out and checked into a downtown hotel along with Burt Cooke, Philip Winslow, and Martin Pratley, Willis's three main diggers and assistants.

Below that, beyond sundry members of the ship's crew—*mustn't overlook them*—nothing. The workers themselves seemed to shun the night life to be had outside the ship.

"Okay. I'm poking around for a while."

Stackman let him through. "Anything specific, sir?"

"No. Just orientation," Slayton lied.

The men inside the huge warehouse were geared for the night, clustering around the steaming coffee urn and chattering in Arabic. They jockeyed empty forklifts with the insane skill of urban Italian drivers, and then trundled them back, loaded, with aching care and slowness.

Base floodlights had been mounted on the high ceiling and positioned strategically on tripods throughout the vast interior. The material was assuming the same general shape as in the hold of the *Star of Egypt*, but here with ruler-straight corridors and breathing space. Another forklift growled past Slayton, leaving the air laden with the smell of greasy machinery, and two men walked by engaged in that form of Hamitic conversation that sounds as if it is about to erupt into a bloody fistfight, but is in actuality merest chitchat. They were weighed down with coils of fat shipping cable, and bound for a huge, disarrayed pile of canvas tarps.

Back near the walls, Slayton checked idly for windows and doors. Since this was a port at which duties were regularly levied, ingress and egress as regarded the warehouses was stringently regulated. He wandered among the debris of dock construction. The warehouse had been cleared out prior to the arrival of the *Star*, though it had been in the midst of building additional facilities for the dock area. Against the wall lay truckloads of construction material. Lumber, cans of paints and chemicals, cinder blocks and such littered the periphery of the neat, secure arrangement of Egyptian cargo.

Slayton checked the ceiling. An acrobat might be able to scale up and across the girder work and undog one of the vents up there. But the man would be obvious in the additional lighting. Maybe, thought Slayton. Maybe, given—of course—a professional.

In the chaotic noise of the warehouse—the basic grating din of men and machinery seemed amplified—Slayton did not notice, at first, the sound of the forklift. It was clearly separated from the main area of activity.

He was standing in the dead end of a dark corridor formed by an eleven-foot-high stack of unused cinder-blocks and bricks on one side, and retired or out-of-service heavy-moving machinery on the other, against a corner of the warehouse.

Slayton heard the independent grumble of a moving forklift, closer to his position than the rest, but could not fix on it. He saw no movement, and the sound seemed pervasive.

Then, above him, the cinder-block wall began slowly to bow outward, toward him.

The first bricks jarred loose from the top of the stack and exploded in gray, dusty chunks to Slayton's left, cutting off escape to the open mouth of the corridor. Each of the damn things weighed at least fifty pounds. As he hugged the warehouse wall, the neat geometry of the stacked blocks wedged outward and collapsed, in an avalanche of gray stone. Choking cement dust rolled up as Slayton fell back, coughing, against an ancient electric cart clotted with black grease, dead and unusable.

If he had taken more than a microsecond to decide and act, he would have had his own pyramid of crushed cinder blocks. Through the dust he saw the twin prongs of a heavy-duty forklift retreat for a second thrust.

He could not leap through the gap—instead, he scrambled up the wall.

Slayton jumped over the chunks of broken brick. The jarring of the line of stacked blocks had disrupted their neat order, and now miniscule hand- and footholds were available on the smooth, stone surface. With mountaineering agility, Slayton countered his own weight against himself, using the momentum that, had he delayed, would have caused him to fall. It required fast coordination of arms and legs, and a single slip would lose the game. The only way to avoid the wall was to go over it.

Which became difficult as the forklift impacted against the stack again. He felt the wall move. The top of the stack was a couple of feet distant, and he struggled to close that gap as he felt the entire wall before him *push* him backwards.

Slayton grabbed a handhold on the top of the stack as the forklift roared and upset the pile. As soon as he got a firm grip with his arms, he repositioned his feet and, as he fell back with the collapsing, disintegrating pile of blocks, he put everything into his legs and pushed off from the wall, arching and twisting across the newly open space.

His timing was good, but of necessity the jump was sloppy. He meant to make the top of a disused tractor provided with a cage for the driver, which was the widest area his fleeting eye could pick as a landing pad. He crashed into the cage sideways, his fingers managing to grip the mesh as momentum wrenched his body around. The pain in his fingers was unbelievable, and he yelled above the noise of the machine. It was doubtful whether the others in the vast warehouse were even aware of what was happening back in that dark corner.

His hold lasted only a necessary second. He came free and landed in a crouch on the now-formidable pile of broken cinder blocks as the forklift backed up for a third run. This time he heard the impact of steel prongs on stone. He saw the row directly in his path of escape begin to tilt.

He leapt clear of the stone debris and ran, full out, under the collapsing wall. It folded down into noisy destruction, filling the spaces as soon as his feet left them, and as he reached the end of the corridor, he dived, sliding on the dirty concrete floor and out into the open.

In a second, Slayton was back on his feet and rushing around the cinder block stack, toward the calculated position of the forklift. He did not regret leaving his pistol behind in the Triumph, as he felt he would not need a gun for what was to come.

The forklift engine was still stuttering away, preparatory to stalling. The machine had been abandoned, tilted slightly by being run onto a pile of the rubble it had produced.

Not cutting speed, Slayton caromed around it, checking back down the corridor he had just left. No movement, nothing. He rechecked the way he had come, and after that, the time lag was too great to allow spotting his assailant. The man possessed excellent diversion and timing sense, and had melted away in the minimum amount of time required.

"Shit," Slayton said to the forklift, reaching in and switching it off. The noise in the warehouse did not decrease noticeably.

He trudged casually back to the area of activity. His business suit was encrusted with sludge and dirt from the warehouse floor, and finely dusted with cement powder. His hands were bleeding freely from the knuckle joints, and he had a scrape on his forehead, which was oozing blood. He became aware of a juicy thumper of a headache slowly swelling behind his left eye.

Slayton felt positive now about the presence, in the group, of Haman. In a strange way, he felt relieved.

The two Arabs with the cable were the first to spot him, and they rushed over, jabbering, offering assistance. One unhesitatingly ripped a sleeve from his sweat-stained workshirt to serve as a makeshift bandage for Slayton's bleeding hands. He accepted Slayton's murmured thanks with a huge smile, revealing teeth edged in brown, and with much exaggerated bowing and talk.

Three more workmen hurried over, two in the wake of a taller man with a classically Arabic hooked nose and a set of blazing, black, diamond-chip eyes. He had high, wide cheekbones and a pointed chin, and among these three points his face assumed a passive, yet somehow gargoylelike expression. But his voice was not high and reedy, like many of his fellows—rather, it surprised even Slayton by being a mellow baritone colored by a faint British accent: "Sir, are you seriously injured? What happened?"

He turned briefly to spray some shotgunned Arabic toward his companions, who retreated, still running an unending row of unintelligible glottals.

"I am Ahmed Sadi. I am in charge of these men. Who among them is responsible for this terrible accident?" His tone seemed to come from another time, a time when impertinence was answered with flogging.

Slayton's voice was a bit rough-edged. "I'm Rademacher."

"Ah, yes, security man. Tell me, Mr. Rademacher, what has happened?" Other curious workers were beginning to drift toward the gathering.

"I have to talk to you," said Slayton.

Sadi barked orders, and the men withdrew to resume their tasks. He and Slayton stood alone in the wide space between the stored artifacts and the area where all the action had occurred scant minutes before.

"Tell me, Mr. Rademacher, can you enlighten me in any way as to your predicament?"

"Ahmed, I need to know about your crew. The men—how much do you know about your crew?"

"Some of them are my brothers. I trust them with my life, and they trust me with theirs. Some are friends of decades. I trust them also."

"Are any of them new, or is there anyone you don't have a lot of background on?"

"Several are comparatively new, but I would not work with strangers."

"Who?"

Ahmed made a gesture of commiseration. "Bassam, Ben Silam, a handful of others. Is it important?"

"Yes."

He thought for a second, and his unusually wide smile split his face again. "It shall be done! Those men will be brought before you and shall not return to work until you are satisfied in your inquiries! There can be no simple compensation for an accident such as this."

"Not exactly true," said Slayton. "None of those men would have a belt on them, would they?"

Ahmed's brow furrowed. "A belt?"

"A drink. Something strong."

"Ah!" His face lit up. He dug furiously within his utility jacket and extracted a tarnished flask, which he uncapped by flipping the lid back with his thumb. He pushed it toward Slayton, who eyed it momentarily, but accepted.

Slayton was expecting something as Arabic as Ahmed's manner, but instead was surprised by the licorice taste. He recognized it at once.

"Ouzo . . . ?" he said, puzzled. It was a fiery Greek liquor, traditionally served cold. "*Warm* ouzo?" He caught his breath.

"My education has taken me to many, many ports, sir," said Ahmed, as if that were some kind of answer.

"Yeah. Well—" The liquor burned its way down and Slayton hesitated, rather than gasping, "—I thank you. I'd like to speak to those men tomorrow morning, when you're finished lugging and stowing."

It took Ahmed a second to catch the idiom. "What? Oh, yes, of course!" He pocketed the flask. "You may question them now, if you wish."

If anyone vanished between now and tomorrow morning, Slayton thought, his job would be even easier. But clear identification was only in the imagination of the attacker; Slayton had not been able to spot the driver of the forklift. No, let the cards play themselves—from now on he was on his guard, primed for anything, including another attempt on his life.

"Tomorrow will be fine," he said. "I've got to go clean up—you understand."

"Of course, sir! I'll see you out."

Together the pair headed back through the warehouse, drawing curious stares and provoking quick bursts of conversation among the workers hefting Egyptian antiquities to and fro.

As Slayton walked, the pain still numbing his face and hands, the cold not helping much, he was brutally aware that Ahmed Sadi, thanks to his magnanimity, had set himself up as a prime suspect. He had the entire work crew under his thumb—they would obviously do anything he ordered them to. He was brash and generous in the way of practiced and clandestine killers; he was a hell-raising Arabic soul gilded with a Cambridge accent and a bizarre taste for Greek liquor. He had the cocky confidence of a man who has had to dispatch several other men in the course of a violent and colorful life—much like Barney Kaufman. Someone with the outward mien of Ahmed Sadi could easily be Rashid Haman.

Slayton's appearance brought raised eyebrows from Stackman, as he passed through, covered with dust and blood.

"Good night Stackman," Slayton said as he passed the checkpoint, and left it at that.

5

"Hello, Wilma?"

"Ben? Ben, is that you? Where are you?"

"Playing with my jolly old computer terminal in Washington, as usual, doing my bit for the national security." Slayton, splayed out chin-deep in a too-small hotel bathtub full of steaming water, languorously draped the washcloth back over his eyes. He knew Wilma's paper had billeted her in a hotel some five miles away, and he had routed his call through Washington, D.C. courtesy of some Treasury Department string-pulling.

"Is that it?"

"No, as usual, I have a favor to ask. Besides what I normally request."

"Smartass."

"Since you're down there covering the Egyptological team, I want to get your impressions of them. Then, when you get back up to the *Post*, I want you to research them. How long would it take you to run up a good accounting of where each of the team's main members came by their experience—in other words, what recommends them for duty like this? Okay?"

Slayton planned to run the team through the computer, and through records, but Wilma's extracurricular research was a way of guaranteeing he would not miss anything outside the normal credits that were sure to surface. She often went beyond the boundaries afforded by cold documentation, turning up interesting and, sometimes, crucial trivia. The long-distance gimmick was a cursory way to insure she would not be on the lookout for him in Baltimore.

"It should take about a day to do it right. I suppose you need this yesterday?"

"As usual. But, say, before the opening of the exhibit."

"You'll have it in two days. I've got stuff to do up here, you know. What do I get for all this selfless effort on behalf of you keeping your employment, anyway?"

Slayton chuckled, the low sound reverberating off the bathroom tiles. "My undying admiration. Important recognition of your singular intellect. All the orgasms you can handle in one session."

"No go unless you throw in dinner, too."

"Where?"

"The Coat of Arms."

"Done." He was smiling, despite his headache.

"I think I've been had," she said, her voice trailing away to indicate that she enjoyed the prospect, at least, of being had by Ben Slayton.

"Appreciate it," said Slayton. "But you know that."

"Don't worry. You're going to work your buns off in recompense."

"Oh, all right," he said in the petulant drone of a chastised schoolboy, and they both laughed.

In fact, Slayton was nearly totally rejuvenated. Later, aboard the *Star of Egypt,* he would hold brief court with Ahmed Sadi's men. He would also be waiting for another contact after last night's, another attempt on his life, if it took that to draw Rashid Haman out. The essence of defeating a trap, thought Slayton, was not avoiding it, but recognizing the danger. If there is a snake in your path, you kill it—you don't forsake the path.

At least, that was the way he hoped it worked.

Four light knocks came on his room door. The tub was steamy and comfortable, and he had almost dozed off. His body woke him up, and a vital second was used in determining whether he had dreamed the knocks, or if they were, in fact, real. After a pause, he heard them again.

He found a towel. The loaded .45 was equally within reach. If this was it, he had to stay off-center from the door.

With the gun in one hand, he spoke around the corner from the closet. "Yes?"

"Mr. Rademacher?" A woman's voice.

"You got him," he said, moving to the peephole. It was Shauna Ramsey.

"Are you busy? May I come in?"

"Just a second!" He dumped the pistol into a drawer alongside a Gideon bible and found his pants. He pulled a fresh white shirt from the closet, and made a point of buttoning a single button, in the middle, after he had opened the door.

Shauna Ramsey definitely did not dress to impress conclaves of solemn archeologists. This morning, she was clad in a fetching black skirt and bolero-vest combination, offset by an elegant golden blouse. One could get lost, Slayton thought, in all that wonderful black hair.

"I've disturbed your bath," she said as a courtesy.

"A welcome interruption, Doctor," Slayton replied, treading carefully. "What's on your mind?"

She appeared suddenly perturbed. "Well—you are involved with the security and safety of the exhibit." She said it as though she was not sure.

"Something the matter?"

"I'm not sure." She moved over to the desk with liquid, graceful strides, and leaned back against it, folding her arms. At last she said, "I think someone has been tampering with the crated artifacts. It's rather nebulous right now—nothing I can specifically put a finger on. But in case I do, I want you to know about it now, and perhaps help me to verify, or deny."

"That does sound rather uncertain."

"We were doing some inspections. Some things are not coming out of the packages the way we put them in. I cannot get more concrete than that right now." She bit her lip.

"I suggest that you show me precisely what is causing the suspicions. You wouldn't be on the alert unless it was something serious." He paused, then looked at her directly. "Would you?"

"Well, I did also want to speak with you. I can give you the official Shauna Ramsey ten-pence primer on Egyptological artifacts. You surprised Gordie, you know?"

"Professor Willis?"

"He's so used to dealing with bumpkins. And I'm up to here, my very eyelids, in dealing with Arabs. You're something of a life preserver, if you know what I mean."

"I love compliments," Slayton smiled warmly back at her. "And you have all of mine. Tell you what: in exchange for your help on the Seth-Olet end of things, I'll give you the underground tour of America's capital city. I'm not as sharp on this stuff as Professor Willis may think."

She was lightly abstracted, looking toward the floor. "I think you'll do well with a quick cribbing session." She was drawn to his rumpled and sexy appearance.

"I'm known for being a quick study," he submitted, sitting conversationally on the bed across from her.

"And I accept the underground tour." She squinted at him in mock gravity. "Is it dangerous?"

"I, madam, am the only survivor of such outings."

"Good. Danger is better than being bored to death." Her tone spoke of midnight dips in cool lagoons and reckless driving on hairpin highways. The magnetism Slayton had recognized on their first meeting was asserting itself as powerfully as ever.

But Slayton thought, business first. Business before. He secured his wayward shirt. "I presume you've breakfasted already?"

"In fact, I've not." It was an enigma to Slayton how such women became scientists, when under the right circumstances everything they said was a suggestion that was more than a bit wanton. Then, he realized the operative phrase was *under the right circumstances*. Given that, everybody was wanton!

"I've only got time for a quick cup of coffee," he admitted, "but you're welcome to share that. Our destinations aren't exactly unrelated, you know." It was true; she had to get to work as well.

"Mr. Rademacher, I thought you'd never ask."

Slayton found time for a quick and discreet check-in call to Winship, during which he recounted his certainty that they were crossing swords with the real Rashid Haman. Winship surprised him by asking him to check in again that evening. "I think some material will be logged in by then that might be of particular interest to you, as relates to Haman."

Slayton neglected to mention the search of his car, or the attack. Everyone so far held potential. Even someone like Shauna might be incriminated by the fact that her overtures to him were growing ever more overt.

Of course, it was also possible that she wished to make up for all the time she had invested in the company of the dead, inside Seth-Olet's *mastaba* in Egypt.

Slayton's interviews with the newer members of Ahmed Sadi's crew were generally a formality, and as such, were unsatisfying. Ahmed insisted on lording over the proceedings like a pharoah's condor, elaborately translating for Slayton. The man named Bassam seemed sullen and hostile, in fact angered, by the indirect nature of Slayton's questioning—a necessity, since he obviously could not dive in, splashing accusations and the magic name of Rashid Haman all over the place at once.

Despite the events of the previous night, Slayton felt an itching, urgent need for action. Something had to break for him soon.

"You are dissatisfied with Bassam, eh?" said Ahmed Sadi, from his corner of the ship's mess.

"I didn't say that," said Slayton.

"You didn't have to. I saw it in your eyes." He got up and approached Slayton, now that the mess was empty, and spoke in an undertone: "Whatever it is you are seeking, my friend, he will not be able to provide you with it. He is merely disgusted with Egyptian politics—he got this job, signed on to get out of the country and away from the problem. He hates the tensions in his country, but at the same time it is his homeland. Do you understand?"

Yes, thought Slayton, *I understand that everyone seems to be incriminated equally but separately.*

"Besides," Ahmed added in an offhanded fashion, "I don't think I've ever seen Bassam operate a forklift. But then, I don't think my men have anything against you, anyway." He shrugged and followed Slayton out of the mess, talking as they went. Ahmed was apparently going to great effort to do a Sancho Panza routine, trailing after Slayton like a squire after his knight.

Up on deck, he peeled away to supervise the crew. The trucks would arrive later in the afternoon, and they would begin loading all over again for the convoy to Washington, D.C. Slayton paused, watching the activity from above, lording over the abstract patterns of movement below, and trying to get spirit messages from it.

Ten to one the information Winship would hand over would be some type of verification. Verification he had already. Now that Slayton had a reason to be alert, it seemed the activity lapsed into a tedious normalcy—which, of course, was the key. Rashid Haman's *crême* of specialties was the art of misdirection. Or, as American military brass had said of the California Japanese during the World War II, "The very fact that there has been no sabotage is an ominous development."

Slayton was stirred out of his reverie by a voice nearby.

"Hey! Whyever are you mooning about up here?" It was the indomitable Maggie Leiber, bundled cozily into a leather coat with a lavish fur mane, which the breeze stirred lazily.

"I've been thinking that people are never who they seem to be," said Slayton.

"Sounds like you might have had a run-in with our own dragon lady," she said, pursing her lips as though she knew in advance how the entire conversation would go.

"You mean Shauna?"

She nodded. "Um-hm."

"You're wrong, Maggie, but I'm flattered anyway."

She hooked his arm in hers. "Walk me down the ramp. Heels can be treacherous sometimes."

He acquiesced gladly. "And just what, *precisely*," he said with theatrical emphasis, "is your role in this circus? Obviously you and Shauna are killing time until the opening."

"Partially true," she said. "I keep the schedules, make sure everyone is where they're supposed to be, generally doing what they're supposed to be doing. I spent all of this morning doing that, and am in fact bound back for the hotel now to further the cause."

"You, a ramrod? But I thought you were a scientist."

"Ah, but I am. My doctorate is strictly archeological, and it helps to know what you're talking about with this bunch. But that's been the extent of it."

"Why?"

Pointedly, Maggie said, "Because I am nowhere near the Egyptologist Shauna is, let alone Professor Willis." The silence hung for a few seconds, and she added, "But you don't have the whole picture. You see, I'm perfectly satisfied with this thing at this moment—it's like a vacation for me. The pressures are normal pressures, not the stuffy emphasis on staying published, on keeping one's academic reputation spotless, and at the same time insuring that you remain in the academic limelight.

"You see, Mr. Rademacher, that kind of pressure kills the pure researchers, the scientists who are in it for the love of the work, the ones you always see on television dressed in the out-of-style clothes. They almost discredit themselves. And one of the reasons I'm working this tour is to act as a buffer between that kind of pressure and Professor Willis."

"It seems to work," said Slayton. "He doesn't really notice anything outside the artifacts." Again, he knew he was lying, but now it was for the purpose of drawing Maggie out.

"He shouldn't be concerned, and isn't. So it's working out, isn't it?"

"What about Shauna?"

"Surely you've noticed how predatory this job has made her. She has good defense mechanisms, but her compensational ones leave a lot to be desired." She trailed off.

"Predatory?" Slayton knew what was coming.

"You mean she hasn't put the make on you yet, Mr. Rademacher? Really." Maggie rolled her eyes.

Near the mouth of the warehouse they stopped and Ben faced her. "And what about you, *Dr.* Leiber?"

"Well, you can only take conversation with the Professor, or with the Arab hoardes over there, so far."

"Funny. That sounds like something Shauna would say."

"We've been in *awfully* close quarters," Maggie said.

"Perhaps you're picking up her . . . um, compensational mechanisms?"

"That sounds like a—what do you call it?—a come-on all by itself, Mr. Rademacher." She smiled, and her eyes literally sparkled.

"Could well be, Dr. Leiber," he said. "I'll see you both at dinner, then."

"Oh, not at that dreadful hotel restaurant, though."

"I think my operatives can produce a suitable local dive."

He left her at the checkout point and headed toward the

warehouse. As soon as she was out of sight, he decided there was really nothing to be gained by another once-over of the place—he knew he would wind up staring at the broken piles of cinder blocks and getting his ear talked off by Ahmed—and turned back toward the checkpoint. If he could catch Maggie, he could buzz her back to the hotel himself.

The lot on the leeward side of the warehouse was deserted; there was only a scattering of parked cars, including Slayton's Triumph. It was almost time to check in with Ham Winship, at any rate.

Out of habit he paused while unlocking the door. No scratches. But the door panel, which he had made a point of buffing clean when he parked earlier in the day, showed several dull fingerprints.

Slayton checked quickly around; apparently the driver's side door had been the only thing touched. He entered the car from the opposite side. Nothing. Once again he checked under the hood.

He saw it instantly.

A packet, wrapped in electrical tape, with a pair of black wires bleeding off to the starter and generator, connected by alligator clips. The packet adhered to the wheel-well on a cushion of military adhesive gum.

His car had, in the parlance of the explosive trade, been "slapped"—that is, an explosive device designed for quick application had been planted. Once under the hood, you slapped it on, connected the wires, closed the hood, and blended into the scenery. Later, when your victim fired up the car, he blended into the scenery as well, but in a more direct fashion.

Slayton gingerly unclamped the clips and jerked the packet loose, smelling its underside to verify the gum and ingredients.

God, what if he had seen Maggie—he might have ushered her into the car without checking, and blown them both to hell! He had proceeded all day long with some unspecified imbalance nagging at him—perhaps this had been it. It was not the sort of gimmick designed for secrecy. He now held it in his hands—intact evidence. Therefore, someone had intended he hurry to his car and jump in, and that meant a phony imperative, to make him hurry.

One of the Sparta men stood across the lot waving his arms, trying to get Slayton's attention.

Slayton fired the Triumph to life, did not explode, and tooled quickly over to where the guard was standing, cranking down the window on the way.

"Yeah?"

"Sir, Professor Willis just phoned from the hotel and said that it was urgent you get over there right away."

"He give any kind of reason?"

"No, sir. I thought I'd flag you in case that's not where you were headed. But that was all he said. Urgent."

"Wonderful," Slayton deadpanned. "Thanks."

6

"Mr. Rademacher, I have absolutely no idea what you mean. Whomsoever phoned the docks, I assure you it was not me." Professor Willis seemed insulted by the suggestion he might need to call for assistance.

Terrific. A planted bomb and a phony phone call to get him into the car with a pretense of urgency. He would have to question the guard. How many of the men knew Willis' voice? How many could slap his car in something under two minutes?

But it was clear, because of the packet now sitting harmless—relatively harmless—in his car, that he had gone from being a nuisance to being a target. Perhaps he should just wire the charge to the driver's side door the next time he left the car in the docks. He might return to find his own target in pieces scattered all over the lot—considering the affection the stranger showed for getting to Slayton via his automobile. Slayton, naturally, took it as a more personal form of affront. He loved his cars.

Willis was not lying. Slayton was certain there was nothing to fear from the Professor. He might have been duped into making the call—but by whom? Tooling slowly, Slayton fixed on a family-style coffee shop he knew to have individual little phone carrels in the back, near the restrooms.

The facilities within were all faceless and gleaming Formica; the waitresses a crew of ebullient, underpaid sixteen-year-olds. If you hit them with anything besides a direct order, they would shake their head as though they were hearing a foreign language. Slayton stopped at the counter to order a black coffee, which he proceeded to take with him toward the telephones.

Slayton slipped into one of the booths and dialed the preliminary clearing number from memory:

Federal Treasury 1-202-566-2000.

"Good morning, U.S. Treasury Department."

"Extension 788, please," said Slayton. Now the maze began.

"Thank you." An extension began to buzz with that blatting, low-frequency ring. Five times.

A click, then tape hiss: "You have reached 788; please insert identification code and clearance number." Click. It was a pleasant, neutral woman's voice.

Slayton dialed 221-121-2212-111, punching the * button between the gaps. They'd have to switch over again when Ma Bell finally found a consumer use for that button.

There was a series of important clicks and relays falling into place, followed by another dial tone, this one high-pitched. Slayton punched in 4-4656. Two buzzes and another woman's voice, this one a live human being, and the final hurdle for Slayton prior to reaching Hamilton Winship on the priority scramble line. "Yes?" was all the voice said.

"Tell Ham we've got to stop meeting like this."

"Mr. Slayton?" The inflection of the voice squeaked upward on the final syllable. That would be Marilyn.

"Marilyn, darling, I have a priority 71 on this. Can you punch me through?"

In response, another line rang, once.

"Slayton?"

"Right."

"Slayton," said Winship gruffly, "I wish to hell you would stop calling me that name, especially to the bloody secretaries."

"What name, sir?"

"I've assembled a briefing for you; I trust you and the tour will be arriving on time."

"Yes, sir. Trucks are being loaded now. We should be late, but we'll be there."

"Any incidents?"

"No sir. Nothing conclusive."

"I'll leave it in your hands, then, and see you tonight."

"Late tonight," said Slayton. It would be good to see if the briefing filled any holes. To Slayton, the attempts on his life equalled a kind of progress, but to inform Winship at this point would be meaningless. *Let's see the briefing.*

"Alright, then." Winship hung up, and there was a fast run of noise that was the priority scramble line disconnecting itself. Winship was unaccustomed to time-wasters like *hello,* or *good-bye,* or *have a nice whatever.* Slayton appreciated that.

He didn't have any scribbles to pocket—to write the numbers down on paper would be professional suicide—and so he left, hitting the counter for two refills on the way back. Perhaps the caffeine would open up some new possibilities in his brain, provide inroads or approaches he had not yet considered that would make everything clearer, or at least, more obvious.

The truck convoy to Washington, D.C., was designed to be slow. It was a stretch of eighteen-wheelers, lead cars, red flags, and blinking lights that frequently backed the traffic up for miles in the no-passing zones. From the sky it would manifest itself as a convoluted mechanical snake, slowly twisting through its wind-up routine.

Ahead of the convoy, Ben Slayton piloted an unmarked government car at a healthy clip nearer the posted limits. There was nothing to be gained by poking along with the trucks—if there was sabotage, for example, he could do little except watch the trucks fall over like groaning dinosaurs—so he had opted to escort the stars of the tour into the nation's capital. Beside him sat Shauna Ramsey, immaculately dressed as usual; behind him, the Professor and Maggie Leiber. Somewhere behind the convoy, Slayton guessed, was Wilma Christian, poking along in her Corvette, doing her best in the name of comprehensive coverage.

"A *mastăba* contains several chambers, Mr. Rademacher, principal of which is a room or chapel in which the actual burial service is conducted," said Willis. "There is a separate compartment in which the body of the deceased is walled off, but it does not contain the corpse—or, if the deceased was better known or wealthier, the sarcophagus. A man's wealth was frequently counted in the number of multiple coffins he could afford, or in the way he was mummified."

"Just like today," said Slayton, and the women laughed politely.

"The compartment features a deep shaft that winds down to another passage that connects to the actual chamber of the dead—the vault. These were often brick-lined, or hewn out of rock, and decorated with paintings depicting scenes from the life of the dead person."

"Except for the poor. I believe they merely tossed them into caves or dug pits for them. Am I correct, Professor?"

"Correct. Their lives did not merit such documentation. Seth-Olet was a soldier, and the vault paintings we have reproduced are quite spectacular. It's hard to scoff, even though I realize there were probably scientists or philosophers, unknown to this day, who were probably dumped in holes with no ceremony, but whose work formed the basis for our present-day science. Money *can* buy you immortality."

"*Reproductions* of the paintings?" said Slayton, momentarily confused.

"Yes," said Shauna. "We couldn't very well ship the entire *mastăba* over to America like the London Bridge. The presentation was Maggie's idea."

Maggie picked up her cue. "We plan to present the artifacts as they would be arranged inside the actual *mastăba,* slightly redesigned to fit onto a horizontal plane, of course. The idea is to present an experience as close to the actual penetration of the tomb as possible. None of your stuffy rows of glass cases here; that's why all the security. Naturally, everything is as tamper-proof as we can make it, as well. But we have huge reproductions of the vault chamber paintings and so on—we want to shut out the outside world as much as possible."

"Except for the TV cameras on behalf of your President," said Shauna, and Willis groaned.

"Oh yes, oh god, the importance of media. The President is to appear live on tape from the tomb of Seth-Olet, to open the tour. Ye gods."

Slayton was inwardly happy. With a minimum of steering, they had worked themselves around to the things he was anxious to quiz them about.

"That means that besides the cameras, your tomb is going to be full of men in natty gray business suits," he said. "I wonder if they'll wear their sunglasses in a tomb?"

Maggie looked confused now. "What?"

Shauna shrugged wearily. "Secret *Service,* love. They're as ostentatious here as Her Majesty's."

"Really," said Slayton, amused.

Shauna stumbled. "Well, that is . . . I've seen a few television shows and they *seem* to be . . ." She actually began to blush.

"What happened to your little car, Mr. Rademacher?" said Maggie abruptly, from the back seat.

"Left it," said Slayton. "No problem. I have several, and couldn't very well fit you three into it for the drive, so my people supplied another. I'll pick it up in a few days."

"Oh," she said, distantly.

Slayton decided not to pursue that topic any further. It was a good excuse to switch to a brief and entirely gratuitous ramble on his car collection. Housed in a special garage on his "farm" in Virginia, the autos ranged from those left to Slayton by his father—Hudson Terraplanes, mostly—to Slayton's own acquisitions, which included his Nash-Healy, Packards from the 1930s, and vintage Cadillacs from even earlier, mainly 1912 through 1920. All were lubricated, rebuilt, as close to mint as Slayton could tinker them, and a good deal of his time on the farm was spent in that garage.

The rap was mainly called up to impress the women in the car, and impress them it did.

"It would be simply marvelous to see all those old cars," said Shauna. "They all work?"

"If they don't work I get extremely perturbed," commented Slayton, ". . . so I spend a lot of time making sure they work. Yes."

"Good for the soul," grumbled Professor Willis, speaking in a low voice like a grizzly bear just grumped up from hibernation. His participation in this conversation had been unexpected to Slayton, though Willis, as usual, seemed to be talking exclusively to himself—the most intelligent audience he could find. "Do the soul good, to see a Packard in good running condition after all these years. Haven't ridden in one since . . . ye gods, since 1938. Only comfortable automobile ever built."

Slayton was taken by surprise, but grinned. It was the first thing he had heard Willis say that was not related to Egyptology, or the tour. He had a fleeting glimpse of a kindred soul; it was not too much of a fantasy to visualize Willis in that garage, clucking over his automobiles.

For now, it would be just fine to get these people rebilleted in a new hotel and see what Winship's briefing had to offer on Rashid Haman—whoever he was. Willis had dozed off in his seat, his pronouncement on Packards the final one, for the moment. Shauna had become mesmerized by the road. She sat distractedly twisting a strand of hair, twining it around her index finger.

At the moment, Slayton was thinking how touchy it might be to search the artifacts comprising the Seth-Olet tour—thousands of pieces—and he decided to cover that, too.

"I hate to bring this up, Shauna, Maggie . . . but those guys in the grey J.C. Penney's suits will want to stick flashlights in rather rude places once all that stuff is uncrated, if the President is going to come anywhere near it. Looking for bombs, revolutionaries, radicals . . . mice . . . anything. Everything makes them nervous."

"Some of the artifacts are extremely delicate," said Maggie immediately.

"Yes. I assume there's some kind of objection to poking into everything, so I thought it would be better to iron this out now. They *will* want to look, and they can be ungracious about it if you have conditions."

"Governmental bully-boys. Why they're called the SS, I suppose," Maggie said to her reflection in the window.

"So," Slayton continued, "I'd like to act as liaison, to supervise the poking, to be the interface, so I can turn one way, shouting at them, then the other, speaking civilly to you. Okay?"

"No objections whatsoever. It would be much more pleasant that way. We've had to deal with insistent spy-types before. Though we've never shot one."

"Though we'd have *liked* to, on occasion," Shauna chimed in.

"No, Mr. Rademacher, you're not like them at all," said Maggie. "Which seems odd."

Uh-oh, Slayton thought. He did not wish to go down *that* road, or provoke quizzes that might undermine his position with the higher-ups of the tour. Instead, he saw another opportunity to shift gears, and seized it: "Washington ahead, ladies."

7

"Then your preliminary investigation has yielded nothing," Winship said, with that downward curl in the sentence that hinted at dissatisfaction with his top man. Slayton naturally had not mentioned the searches, bombs, or assassination attempts he had been subjected to over the past couple of days.

"On the contrary, sir," he said, standing before Winship's desk with his hands clasped behind his back. "I'm in especially tight with the three principal members of the contingent. My contact for the Arab workers turns out to be their leader, and he's most anxious to please. If there is any indication that there will be an incident," he was careful to add, ". . . of *any* type, not only do I now have full cooperation of the people who matter, but several prime suspects among the crew."

Winship sat and absorbed the information. The pipe came out and he began fiddling with it, waiting for more.

"Frankly, sir," Slayton cleared his throat, "if Haman was to make any move involving the tour, it would be stupid to do it in Baltimore. If we're going to see any actions on his part, it will more likely be in Washington."

"Why, if he is so thorough?" asked Winship.

"Because he's also a prima donna, sir. He involves himself with theatrical plans and grand-slam staging for his gimmicks. He has the stealth for the unobtrusive setup, sure, but he'll get gradually more obvious as deadline time approaches."

"An unfortunate choice of phraseology."

"What I mean is that *now* is the time to look for Haman's presence, not when he's in Baltimore."

"In that case," said Winship, "I have several things here that ought to provide you with a very good reason to stay alert nights when everyone else is sleeping."

Slayton decided to keep the comment that came to mind exclusively to himself.

"First, Shafter in Egypt reports that Haman definitely left with the Seth-Olet tour. If he's not with the tour, then he came over with it, and we might have had him at the docks—"

"No sir. You're underestimating Haman, again."

Winship harrumphed, looking dourly up from the scattered papers on his desk. Slayton shut up, and he continued: "Second, we have reason to believe that although you have not yet identified Haman, he has identified you. So much for infiltration."

"Is that concrete, sir?" said Slayton, hoping Winship did not know about the incidents and was just stringing him along.

"Not ironclad, but the third thing is," shot back Winship. "Records reveal that three years ago you inadvertently got mixed up in one of Haman's spoiling raids and killed three of his men. If the man is Haman, and if he has the make on you as we suspect, and *if* he makes this connection, then you might be in greater danger than the President." Winship let that hang while Slayton provided the missing part.

"But, Ham—I'm already committed to protect the President during this thing. And we both know the limits of that commitment, so the best I can do is try to get Haman before he gets me." His voice was deadly and neutral. Winship did not have to be told the side-effects of the game, but Slayton felt the urge to lay them out in detail.

"And if Haman gets me, I think we can both give up on the President."

Winship puffed thoughtfully on his pipe, meeting Slayton's eyes directly only for a second as he spoke.

"I should have better faith in the men I would assign to replace you," he said. "But I think you're right, though I'll call you a liar if you were to tell anyone else."

"Anything else on Haman," asked Slayton, slightly embarrassed and returning to business.

"The international computers don't take any more time than the domestic ones. All are damn short on details, except for descriptions of the raids Haman participated in; assassinations, torture, murder . . . and of course, lists of the dead. Which is why you have to watch your step, Ben." Rarely did Winship use Slayton's first name in this fashion.

"Haman is particularly ruthless in the matter of retribution. He once uncovered a spy in his own group, a plant from a French group of corporations he was in charge of blackmailing. He promptly delivered a personal demand for twice the amount he had tried to extort previously—a demand that went directly to each company head, accompanied by a piece of the dead agent. His hands, his ears, his testicles . . . there were quite a few executives." He let the implications hover in the space between himself and Slayton. "They paid."

"So if Haman places my handsome face, I can say hello to the meat grinder. Except for one thing: I don't really think Haman placing me would be allowed to leak unless Haman wanted me to know he knew me."

"I don't follow."

"He's throwing the gauntlet down, daring me to stop him. Of course we could cancel the tour, lock the President in a bank vault somewhere. But to Haman that's a chicken-hearted response. Fear is what allows him to operate freely. Cancelling the tour would in itself be a propaganda victory of sorts. If we *don't* panic, and accept the challenge, we have a better chance of getting him."

Winship's expression rearranged into horror at the prospect of setting up the President of the United States, which is what Slayton seemed to be getting at.

"Wait, sir, wait. Now—Haman loves to be the victor, not just to do a job you could hire any thug for. It's his style. It's why his attacks are flamboyant and successful. He prefers hunting a cougar with a bowie knife and winning, rather than insuring his win by shooting carp in a beer barrel, if you follow my analogy."

The expression subdued itself, just slightly.

"If you'll pardon me, sir, I think Haman knows that I am about as proficient as he is. It's a dare. Or rather, a wager—the winner gets the President."

"Jesus H. Christ on a *crutch*, Slayton!" Winship had absently gathered the papers into a neat stack on the desk, hinting that the exchange was finished on a factual level. "Your duty is to protect the President at any cost, not to trifle with his life to even some obscure, stupid score!"

"Exactly, sir. And I think a moment ago I mentioned that I understood the depth of that commitment. Trust me."

Winship snorted, calmed down a bit by now. Slayton made for the office door, turning for a parting shot.

"And you'll see me after this, sir, and I'll still be in one functional piece." The door hissed shut with a thump.

The dour expression had become resigned. "I hope so, Benjamin," the man behind the desk said. "Sincerely."

Slayton spent a while with a pot of coffee and the stack of documentation, soaking up specifics on Rashid Haman's diverse inventory of atrocities. It was entirely possible that, despite the events of the last two days, Slayton had had no direct contact with the terrorist.

He would have operatives waiting in the United States, people who would follow his orders—providing one of the best ways to execute hits and gimmicks. Fly them in, and if they live through the gimmick, fly them out. But don't pick them off the local trees. The British authorities had wasted months after the gimmick that bumped off a pair of Cabinet members, rounding up and grilling locals, when Haman had shipped in one of his star students, a Japanese now supervising terrorist phalanges in his home country. While the British were convicting a couple of wackos who happened to have antigovernment diaries, the Oriental was enjoying a drink on the plane home. Now, like Haman, this man also farmed out work for money whenever he needed folding cash.

Which brought up another ugly point, which became even more apparent as Slayton delved into the new dossiers: Haman was no patriot. He needed a formidable cash-flow to maintain his nonprofile, to hide, to set up and execute gimmicks. Often, officials had to be bribed on an international basis, and that required lots of money. Thus, it was entirely likely that Haman's choice of America had a twofold motivation. Not only was somebody paying him to set up the President and embarrass the government in front of the Egyptians, but somebody else was forking over for his services as a teacher of home-grown guerillas. Plus, Slayton's subconscious nagged, there are probably four or five other reasons you haven't thought of yet.

The Seth-Olet tour was setting up in Washington, D.C., and the head count among the crew and supervisors remained constant. If Haman was there, he had not disappeared on the docks.

Of course, he would know the government could identify the work of Rashid Haman, and that would make it necessary to leave the country as soon as possible. To Haman, the best way to vanish from a country was to stay inside its borders. You either escaped within seconds, or stayed around to watch the guys with the diaries get grilled on national television. Either way, you did not get caught, and that was the basis of the bigger game.

Slayton did not make a habit of smoking, but he wanted a cigarette now. He needed some philosophical smoke drifting around him.

Terrorists had no ideals; they played both sides of political shortcomings against the middle, usually killing the innocent in the interest of point-making for people or systems they would just as easily turn on, killing for whoever would pay the asking price. Politicians fought wars, killing the innocent to perpetuate the international shell game. Revolutionaries and anarchists killed the innocent for causes. Deaths were totalled in different coinage, but the result was still death. Haman specialized in death, in spreading the madness, and it was Haman and people like him who had brought the United States to the brink of the same type of urban terrorism that now determined railway schedules in Ireland, or curfews in Jordan.

He pushed back from the desk. The records room was too well-lit, like a classroom, conducive to reading but not to thinking.

He glanced at his watch, a Seiko which he had retained, sweep hands and all, throughout the craze for electronic digitals. It was midnight, and it was time to contact Wilma, to see if she had come up with anything on the histories of the tour people.

Slayton stepped out of the building.

"I've got an absolute ream of notes," Wilma told him over the phone. "I'd rather pass 'em to you under a table than read the entire novel over the telephone."

"Done and done," said Slayton, and they arranged to meet at Wilma's apartment.

Driving, Slayton felt a residual twinge of anxiety. He was certain he was not being followed, yet, if Rashid Haman was on his tail—as his paranoia did not insist, but *suggested*, with its sly, used-car dealer's grin—it would be idiotic to endanger anyone else, let alone anyone close.

Somehow Slayton felt he would live through the night. He also knew, as did Wilma from the moment she picked up the phone, that it would be impossible to merely scoop up the folder-full of her painstaking amateur detective work and breeze out of the apartment. The idea that he might get murdered had nothing to do with terrorists.

She met him with a glass of wine, and his fears were confirmed. But first, she insisted, "I have to tell you about the Egyptological swap meet that's coming to our fair town." Slayton smiled pleasantly, and braced himself for a dunning repetition of facts he had known for some two days.

"It seems that the barge that brought these priceless artifacts to our shores—it's called the *Star of Egypt*, fittingly enough—may also have unloaded a second cargo of god-knows-what."

"What?"

"Take a look," she said, trotting to the sofa with a manila folder of 8×10 glossies. She dropped it in his lap. The positives were heavily grainy.

"Are these blowups?" said Slayton.

"Yeah. Unfortunately I had to use my James Bond camera." It was the way she referred to her 16-mm subminiature Minolta. She saw him squinting, and leaned closer, pointing. "The men unloading the boxes are Americans. The trucks—there were two—checked out as rentals out of Albany, New York."

"Where is this?"

"Okay, only orientation I could get was against the boat. Ship, I mean. Here." She pointed out several shots that emphasized a warehouse door, a garage-sized affair set into a cul-de-sac beyond the rear portion of the *Star of Egypt*. Beyond that, Slayton could make out, in fuzzy relief, what had to be the cordoned-off section of the docks where the Seth-Olet tour had unloaded.

He felt like smacking his head. Right next door!

"What do those boxes tell you, Ben?"

He saw no point in lying. "They look to me like grenade crates, crates for M-16's or LAW rockets." He stopped and looked directly at Wilma. Her enthusiasm flagged just slightly.

"I know, I know," she said. "Which brings it into the jurisdiction of not only the Bureau of Alcohol, Tobacco and Firearms, but also U.S. Customs, which both translate as Treasury, which translates as you . . . and do I have to give up my pictures?"

She and Slayton had had this conversation before, in varying degrees of seriousness, throughout their relationship. But he needed whatever else she had.

"I'd like to take them, but not for the reasons you think. These could help me immensely. So," he piled them back into the folder and placed the folder between them, ". . . let's skip the part where you deny having duplicates, okay? Otherwise you wouldn't bait me by asking if you could keep them."

"Rats," she said. "You rise so eagerly to the offered carrot, you know, and sometimes it's fun to watch. I knew I was onto something." But she did not yet feel the piercing sense of urgency that Slayton was contending with. "They're yours," she said.

"On one condition," Slayton finished.

She looked taken aback. "No way. I've got several. First board: exclusive story rights if and when."

That was normal, and Slayton nodded, as usual.

"Second board: I'm not going to stop my investigation just because you're starting yours."

"Fair enough." She would, anyway.

"Third board: you've got to tell me what you know about that ship in exchange before I give you what I've got on the passengers. I have a sneaking feeling they're connected somehow."

She had watched him react to the photographs, and the reactions to the shots of the dock area were mainly ones of familiarity. She, too had skipped steps in the conversation. The dazzling blue eyes were all business.

"Alright," Slayton said simply. "For that I'll need time, though."

Wilma had heard that one before, so she said, "Word of honor."

"Uh-oh, caught again. Okay. I promise, alright?"

"Fine." She excused herself, presumably to dash to the bathroom.

He returned his attention to the pictures. Perhaps there had been a door, or egress of some kind, behind the junked machinery. It would surely provide for the quick escape of the assailant he never had gotten the chance to identify. What if Seth-Olet crates had been removed from one part of the warehouse to an adjacent section, all the time men were loading and unloading?

It made elementary sense, if one could see past the fact there were some thirty workers and guards in the Seth-Olet section, none of whom were asleep. Seth-Olet boxes could be taken next door, broken down, and trucked away while everyone's attention was on the safety of the artifacts.

Shauna Ramsey had noticed tampering with some of the crates, and consulted him.

He grimaced into the maddeningly fuzzy photographs. Somewhere in there were the faces of Rashid Haman's domestic army, his trainees. Still, it was an unexpected windfall of sorts. More verification he did not need, after this.

Wilma reappeared, wrapped in a trench coat. "Tell me, Mr. Slayton, would the image you see before you pass muster as, shall we say, an unobtrusive spy-sorta person, someone who could blend into the scenery and operate unnoticed, like, for example, a Treasury agent?"

"Have you filled out an application?" he said, deadpan.

"No. But I have excellent references."

"Unfortunately, tops on our list of qualifications is *not* the question, *do you have your own trenchcoat?*"

"Darn."

"Do you have any more conditions?" he asked, indicating the folder beside him on the couch.

"One more." She nodded soberly.

"I'm waiting," he said.

"Do you really think I wouldn't make a good secret agent?"

"Secret agent, I don't know. Treasury agents don't wear secret agent trenchcoats, though."

"I know *tae-kwondo*. I can shoot."

"I know."

"I have a spy camera. I've seen all the James Bond movies," she added, mock-desperately. "Twice."

Slayton folded his arms, administratively silent.

"Guess I ain't cut out for the life, huh?"

Slayton struggled to look like Winship in one of his gruff, bureaucratic moods. He cleared his throat importantly and nodded.

"Shit."

"That's what all the applicants say," intoned Slayton.

"Grounded before I even took off," she said, petulantly yanking the trenchcoat belt out of its loops and throwing it on the floor. She whipped off the coat and tossed it over Slayton's head.

She did not have anything on underneath the coat, and Slayton recognized the essence of her final condition—Board Number Four, as it were.

"Wait a minute," she said as he pulled her down into the sofa. She unfastened his shirt and pants in record time.

"What is it?" he said against her mouth, trying to work at two or three things at once.

"The pictures," she said, dropping the folder to the floor. "Don't want to crush them."

He was already mostly stripped. "Good thinking, Mister Bond." Her body melted onto his, and they fit together very well indeed. Practice was everything.

Slayton managed to fulfill all of Wilma's conditions.

8

The uncrated artifacts were fabulously beautiful. They glowed, unlike rotting shards of pottery or dead silk, centuries old. Some of the items looked newly minted, as gleaming and dazzling today as forty centuries ago. Slayton caught his breath in fascination.

And through the tableau moved a figure from another time, an enchanting woman with flowing dark hair. She might have been a court dancer from the Pharoah's stable, or some kind of concubine indoctrinated in the arts that drive men wild and cause thrones to fall. Here, she touched a golden jug in passing; there, caressed the flank of a glittering sarcophagus.

Slayton saw how easily Shauna Ramsey fit into the strange jigsaw of Egyptology. It had the power to hypnotize beautiful women, to fascinate them in the *real* sense of the word, perhaps through the cat god, Bast, and the basilisk gaze that that particular daughter of Isis offered the mute world.

"See how it all shines!" She was enraptured, enthusiastic. "This is the general arrangement, though everything is still scattered around. Finishing touches come up until the last moment—Professor Willis is forever rearranging things in the interests of historical accuracy; then Maggie changes them around to fit her concept of a more effective presentation."

"The mummy goes here?" indicated Slayton, somewhat like a perturbed housewife unable to decide where to place the new piano.

"The sarcophagus area. The multiple coffins go inside, and the whole package goes here. Now—" she looked around,

"—near the sarcophagus go the Canopic jars; those are these." She lifted an ornate jug to the light and it glittered. "Important for several reasons. First, almost all the *mastăbas* found previously were pre-Dynastic, which means they date to an era that wasn't known for flashiness and ostentation."

"All this elaborate, throw-away stuff came in with the pyramids, then? Disposable gold?"

"Roughly, yes. You know what Canopic jars are, don't you?"

What was taking place was a quiz every bit as elaborate as the tomb furnishings Slayton was inspecting. His rudimentary Egyptological knowledge was having its limits tested by Shauna—since Slayton had dropped a ringer on Willis earlier—and Slayton was in turn quizzing Shauna, rationalizing that he had not yet pinned *her* to the wall, testing her in his subtle fashion to see if she was in fact what she claimed to be. It was time, and the touchy game proceeded.

"Supplied for the storage of the intestines of the dead," said Slayton. "Literally, guts. But heart, liver, and so on, too, all supposedly to be restored in the Afterlife."

"But *these* Canopic jars indicate that Seth-Olet was treated to the most expensive form of *qes*, because under the cheaper methods, the organs were dissolved."

"How expensive was all this?"

"One talent of silver. In 1904, that equalled about £240, or . . . I'm lousy at mathematics. . . ."

"Around six hundred bucks. Six hundred 1904 bucks," Slayton said. "Still pretty costly. What did you get for your money?"

"You got your brain removed through your nose with a pair of iron forceps," said Shauna. "Then you were slit open—by Guild practitioners, of course, all this being done strictly according to law—with a sharp Ethiopian stone. Your intestines were removed, cleansed in palm wine, salted with aromatic gums that had been beaten into powder, and placed in the jars."

"Good idea," said Slayton, who knew from bitter experience what a freshly slit-open corpse smelled like.

"*Then,*" Shauna said, moving to several jars decorating a counter top, "your body would be filled up with myrrh and cassia—and anything else that was astringent and smelled good—and then laid in natron for seventy days. Natron is a sodium carbonate, hydrated, and it certainly killed any odors that were left. But after they removed you, they washed you again anyway. Then you got wrapped up in linen strips smeared with gum—three or four hundred yards-worth of bandages. That's just for openers."

"Do tell," said Slayton.

There was mischief in Shauna's eyes. "Okay, you asked for it. Come over here, I want you to see this stuff so you don't think I'm making this all up."

Slayton obliged, and found himself at a desklike table scattered with yet-uncataloged odds and ends. He held up a small, heavy image of a man in repose.

"I think this is called a *cartonnage,* isn't it?" The work appeared very intricate. "What's it made out of?"

"Twenty to forty layers of that linen, glued together, a lot like pasteboard, then covered with stucco. The coloring is tempera; the inscriptions are the names of deities and things from the Book of the Dead. You find the Book of the Dead everywhere; apparently, the more times you mentioned it on your burial items, the better chance you had at the Afterlife."

"What do you do with this?"

"It goes inside the wrappings. You find all sorts of things wrapped up with the mummy—porcelain bugles, images of gods, and of course, chapters from the Book of the Dead."

"An ominous title, like the *Necronomicon.*"

"Actually closer to a combination of *Frankenstein* and the Bible. It was called *Per em hru,* 'the chapters of coming forth by day,' a collection of burial-related chants. Sort of a hymnal of chapters regarding the dead."

More little figurines like the *cartonnage* lay to one side, and Slayton browsed over them.

"Those are *Ushabtiu* figures, old kings, generally—to do services for the dead. They were made out of everything—wax, clay, stone, wood, porcelain—and the inscriptions—"

"More Book of the Dead?"

"Right. They were placed all around the coffin, like the Canopic jars. But the most important little guy was this one, placed in the coffin with the mummy, or actually wrapped up in the bandages."

Slayton lifted a wooden figure carved onto a thick base, almost like a coffee-table statue.

"That's a *Ptah-Seker-Ausår* figure. A triune god—do you know the components?"

"Uh—" Slayton wracked his memory; the names were familiar from his quick research. "Uh—*Ptah* . . . the creator. *Seker* was the god of death. *Ausår* was another name for . . . um, Osiris, god of resurrection and therefore, immortality."

The little figure wore horns, a sun disk, and plumes on its tiny head to verify each of Slayton's descriptions.

"There's a little drawer there in the base," said Shauna. "That's the special part; it contained a papyrus roll with colored vignettes of the mummy's life and—"

"And more Book of the Dead," Slayton added, obviously pleased with himself as well as with his vindication of the woman doggedly describing everything in detail to him. Somehow she had sensed that he needed convincing.

"As for the other stuff near the coffin—" She indicated it with a sweep of her hand. "—those are all vessels of one type or another, to hold food, wine, unguents, whatever viands the mummy might need . . . you must include items that the mummy used while living, or prized, or just liked, and in Seth-Olet's case that means we have a lot of ancient weaponry cluttering up the coffin area . . . then you have gifts from the relatives and friends, which include little insignificant things, like chariots—of which we have one, right over there—battle armor, pets—which means everything from mummified dogs and cats to horses . . ."

"God, if we did this that way today," said Slayton, "it would mean about half the gross national product would go underground every year."

"It's a fad that's difficult to explain to a starving population," offered Shauna.

"Spectacular, though. And much more involving for the people who knew the deceased. But I'm afraid I don't have that many friends who'd be willing to chant and sing at my funeral."

"I don't have that many friends, period," said Shauna. "But, according to the beliefs, your Afterlife was literally in their hands. Your friends and the priests were supposed to compose prayers and short litanies, all of which made reference to your 'future life.' The readings of these were all-important; they guaranteed you unhindered passage to God in the next world, allowed you to overcome ghostly foes, would allow your corpse to resist corruption, and ensure you a new life, in a glorified body, up there." She jerked her thumb toward the ceiling.

"God help you if your friends wanted to screw you up," summarized Slayton.

"It's all a classical romantic notion," she said. "A lost age. You'll pardon my rambling. Sometimes I wonder if I won't end up like Professor Willis."

"Bloody impossible," said Slayton.

"I like the way you handled it," she said, her face turned so that it was in darkness and the light shone on her cascade of hair. "It took you about ten minutes to get over my body and start talking to me professionally."

Slayton came to attention. "It's not a routine, and I'm not that mechanical. I haven't gotten over your body *yet*."

"A battle between the physical and mental *personae*. My apologies. We've been working a lot. The last thing I expected to have on this tour was a sexual identity problem. There was room in the Egyptian god-hierarchy for women, you know—every important god had a female counterpart or alter ego. They were sexually interchangeable, unlike the Greeks or Romans where the distinction between god and goddess was sexist." Her words had dwindled into a kind of frustrated bitterness.

He said it too fast, but got it out: "Shauna, can I help at all?"

There was a long and decisive silence, then: "Yes. Yes, I think you might be able to." She reached across the table, taking his hands, pulling him toward her, wrapping her intoxicating body and scent in the warmest of embraces. Slayton held her that way for several minutes, and when she had dammed back brief tears, she brought her head up from his shoulder and kissed him thoroughly and hungrily, as though she were drawing sustenance from his body. It lasted quite a long time. She made small sounds of pleasure.

And when she looked back at him her eyes were shining blackly, promising dancer's eyes, and she said softly, "I'd like to see Washington, now."

By ten o'clock that evening, Ben Slayton had managed to shake the untidy notion that Rashid Haman might be Shauna Ramsey. The new possibility that Haman might be a gestalt personality—that is, several people instead of a single man—was his new theory, but it, too, was quickly discounted. Haman's blueprints, and gimmicks, bore the stamp of an individual. To Slayton's perception, egomania was easily added to the incomplete picture of that personality. Besides, if Haman were more than one person—a group, say—then someone still had to make decisions, give orders . . . he could not visualize a terrorist phalange being run like a San Francisco commune of the late 1960s, with community decisions overriding everything.

No, these notions were annoying sideroads, tossed into Slayton's path to force him to waste time in fruitless pursuits, while elsewhere, plans were being laid and actions taken. Misdirection was Haman's forte. He seemed to be a man of many parts.

"A man in ancient Egypt was composed of nine distinct parts," said Shauna, intruding on the subtext of Slayton's thought.

"That sounds like a dirty joke."

"No, it's true. There's your *khat;* that's your physical self. Your corruptible body."

"Leave my corruptible body out of this," he said, waggling a Groucho Marx eyebrow. "I don't have many faults, but I make the most of the ones I *do* have."

The devastated remains of their dinner filled the table before them, and periodically their waiter recharged their glasses and kept them happy. The food at Haskell's had always been secondary to the service, but all in all it was an entertaining choice.

"Now, there's also your *sāhu,* spiritual body, and *åb,* your heart—heart in the sense of the seat of life and thought."

"Sort of like id, ego, and superego."

"Rather, yes. Then there's your *ka* and your *ba.*"

Slayton could not hold back the laugh that welled up. "I'm sorry," he said, going for his napkin.

"This is serious business," she chided. "*Ba* is literally your soul. *Ka* is your double, an abstract sort of essence of individuality. *Ka* is endowed with your personality, all of your characteristic attributes—in your case, that redolent sense of humor—and it has an *absolutely independent existence.* They thought one's *ka* could inhabit a statue of the deceased, another reason for all the figurines."

"But, if I get blown away by someone, I don't even have a statue. The closest thing I have is an inflatable doll in the bottom drawer of my dresser."

Shauna cleared her throat like a teacher admonishing a naughty schoolboy, continuing, "You also have a shadow, a *khaibit;* a wispy sort of intelligence or similitude called *khu*—a 'shining' is a good word for it—and a *sekhem,* a divine form." This time, Shauna laughed.

"I'll thank you not to giggle at my divine form, madam. So that's what little Egyptian boys are made of."

"One more thing," she said.

"Oh, *no,*" said Slayton. "I think I've heard this before."

"Will you *listen,* please. It's not what you think. It's *ren.* Your name." She grasped his hand across the table. "Whatever your name really is, Ben."

"Like cats," Slayton changed the topic, once again reinforcing his awareness of the things going on around him, keeping his body in perpetual condition yellow—alert, but relaxed.

"Cats are said to have three names: the name by which people call them, the name by which other cats call them, and the private name that cats call themselves, which no one ever finds out."

"And which are you, Benjamin? Benjamin Rademacher." She sounded ill at ease saying it, as though some muse told her it was not real.

"I'm the man getting us the hell out of here, because you and I have had exactly enough to drink, and we both have frightful workloads to face tomorrow which must not be compromised."

"You're right. But tonight isn't finished yet, either. I'd be a sad specimen of a woman if I dragged you out and liquored you up and then spent the night alone, cataloging the various parts and names of various people." She was still smiling.

"Verily, the road to lunacy."

"Verily, sir. If you don't make love to me of a passionate nature, I shall become quite cross with you." She assumed a stern expression. "Don't argue. You're doing your job. You're protecting the Seth-Olet exhibit and keeping the members of the tour happy."

"Well, since you put it that way . . ."

9

In Washington, Shauna Ramsey had wound up with a suite, which to her was a vast improvement over the cramped hotel room she had shared with Maggie Leiber in Baltimore, or the confined cabin aboard the *Star of Egypt*. She told Slayton so.

"Well, I don't know about you, but *I'm* pleased," she said, rolling toward Slayton on the huge king-sized bed. She was luxuriously wound up in the sheet, almost mummified, her hair in glorious disarray, her body smelling warm and familiar. She pulled herself onto Slayton's chest and propped her head on a fist.

"This place is like Haskell's," she said. "The service is terrific. Smashing. Etcetera."

"This is intermission. The show's not over yet," Slayton said from the back of his throat.

"Are you going to talk to me now, sir?"

"Hm?"

"I've been waiting all evening for you to tell me what on earth is bothering you. Are you going to keep playing diversionary games, or are you going to let me help you a little bit?"

It did not take Slayton long to ponder her offer. "There is a man, part of your tour. My department—which is not important—wants him. So far he could be anyone on the tour, but I'm fairly convinced he's one of those faceless Arab workers."

Naturally she was interested—she had gotten what she wanted. "Who is he, Ben? What has he done?"

Slayton's eyes were focused in the darkness somewhere beyond the foot of the vast bed. "He's an international terrorist. He's killed maybe a hundred and fifty, two hundred people by himself. He's been responsible for the deaths of hundreds more. His students and stunt gangs have murdered thousands in the name of terrorism.

"He came here on the *Star of Egypt.* He got here just in time to supervise the unloading of what I'm sure are smuggled weapons. He has eyes on the President of the United States, and I am convinced he'll use the tour to get to the President. I have to find out who he is and stop him. And so far, not too much luck. But I know he's here. And I'm going to get him. I hope he's ready."

Her expression took on tones of serious shock. "Ben . . ." The words failed her for a moment. "Good god, I didn't have any idea . . ."

"And no, I'm not kidding."

They remained in silence for a few moments, each assimilating the new patterns of thought. Though Slayton's new trust in Shauna was elementary, he was convinced she could offer some tidbit, some inconsistency which would unlock the puzzle for him. Anything she could call forth was important. The details on the nine components of mortals was a fundamental part of Rashid Haman's ancestral past—perhaps he was tapped into that mythology somehow, perhaps he could be predicted, Slayton theorized, along the lines of genetic vice. Damn it all, this was his own specialty! In a word, his calling was troubleshooting. Defeat from someone like Haman was unacceptable.

Shauna sensed that what Slayton needed most were details, raw material with which to work, like the background research, or Wilma's dockside photography.

"Those tampered boxes suddenly seem awfully important," she said. "You'll see them tomorrow, I suppose."

"Tonight," said Slayton. "I think now is the best time for this sort of thing."

It took her no time at all. "Agreed," she said, pulling herself up and kissing him again. "We'll get back to this later."

She began to bounce off the bed, but Slayton caught her arm in the dark. "Wait a minute."

"What . . . ?"

"Shhh!" Slayton was scanning the room furiously in the dim light. He pulled her by the arm, back onto the bed, laying his palm against her in a silent entreaty to stay right where she was as he slowly rose, naked and vulnerable.

She saw him, the bluish glow through the closed curtain illuminating his tight, hard-muscled frame. He took slow and cautious paces, head darting around at what she imagined might be small noises that perhaps she could not even hear. He was near the foot of the bed, his arms extended, fingers spread, treading carefully.

What Shauna Ramsey saw next must have looked pretty amazing.

Ben Slayton seemed to shoot up and out, straight up into the air, then flying out sideways, flipping, coming down on his shoulders a good distance from the bed, and rolling efficiently to a combat crouch some ten feet from the bed. She started to move, but his voice rang out in the darkness.

"Stay right where you are, Shauna! Don't move a muscle!"

He smacked the light switches in the far corner of the suite's bedroom with the heel of his hand, and at once lights blazed on near the door, on the desk, and beside the bed. At the same time, at the foot of the bed, Shauna saw a flat black, reptilian snout poke tentatively up. It weaved skittishly, a forked tongue of pale pink underlaid with black mottles, testing the air.

Her jaws cemented together and her entire body tried to shrink back against the headboard. It was a massive effort just to turn her head because of the trembling that had overcome the muscles in her neck. The thing was close enough for her to discern the square patterns of scales surrounding its nostrils and the almost imperceptible juncture of its mouth and jaw. The tongue slithered in and out of the tiny gap below the nostrils. Within that mouth were the fangs, short and lethal.

Slayton cast frantically around for a weapon, an object with which to put distance between himself and the huge snake now partially on the floor and climbing up the bed. The damned thing was a monster, black as death and fully as big around as the wine bottle which lay somewhere on the floor to Shauna's left, now empty.

He tried to seize the desk lamp, but it was bolted to the table. The desk chair was heavy and unwieldly, but there was no time, and it was the only object at hand. Most of Shauna's luggage and possessions were unpacked in the adjacent room of the suite.

He rushed across the room, thinking two things, and fighting to balance them. The swing would be all biceps, he would instinctively extend his arms full-length no matter how he planned it, since his body was reflexively intimidated by the sheer size of the creature before him. That, and considering the girth of the thing and the musculature that size implied, the impact of the chair might not faze it too much.

But it was slithering closer to the terrified Shauna, and that gave him the adrenalin he needed.

Slayton swung the chair in a sweeping arc across the top of the bed. His charge had brought his feet within inches of the coiled body still on the floor.

He lucked out, clipping the snake's massive skull with one of the lower chair legs, propelling it partially off the big bed. Momentum betrayed him, and he followed the heavy chair, losing his balance and falling sideways onto the bed. The mattress bounced thickly. As he fell, tilted at an angle, he saw the snake's head rise in mid-air, recovering from the force of the blow. It began to crank around toward him.

Slayton used what falling momentum he had left to push himself further up on the bed, far enough to grasp Shauna's arm in a viselike grip and employ an elementary push-and-pull judo tactic to throw her clear of the bed on the side opposite the snake. She cried out in pain as her arm was unceremoniously wrenched, but now she was clear, scrambling naked toward the door connecting the rooms of the suite.

For Slayton, it was too late. If he jumped, his leg would be pegged by a pair of fangs. Was cobra venom the type that turned your brain to jelly, or the kind that paralyzed your nervous system, suffocating you? It did not matter. The hood was aggressively extended full-out. The head, like a tank turret, weaved for a good strike position mere feet distant. Slayton could not take his eyes off the thing.

His right arm scooped up a pillow and thrust it forward just in time to deflect the first strike. Slayton had not seen it coming—it was so *fast*—but his body could not remain frozen. The serpent gaffed into the pillow and instantly withdrew, resuming its striking stance, looking for a new opening, like a hungry boxer.

Slayton held the pillow defensively, trying to cover the maximal striking area. When it lanced out again, there was a microsecond in which Slayton knew the strike was coming, and he reacted instantly. As the head blurred into motion, he managed to swat it to the left by swinging the pillow.

Like a taut, expensive armature, the head began to rebound, almost arrogantly, convinced of its structural superiority. But by that time Slayton's other hand had come into play, one-two, and tossed the sheet over its head as the third strike came, and the snake, momentarily disoriented, landed near Slayton's thigh.

He clamped his hand down on the shape under the sheet, fervently hoping he was close enough to the head to avoid it coiling double and biting his hand. All bets were off.

If he could not maintain a stranglehold on the thrashing head and body, it would be the end.

Holding its head under the sheet, feeling the creature bunch and writhe in his grip, Slayton came to his knees and rolled off the far side of the bed, dragging the snake with him, stretching its body rigid and straight for a brief second. He thumped onto the floor. Coils looped over the bed and twined around Slayton's naked legs as the incredibly powerful thing flopped around in his grip, which, thanks to the sheet, was losing ground fast.

The empty wine bottle was wedged beneath his leg. He found the neck and yanked it out.

He pushed the shape down to the carpet as the coils cinched tightly around his legs, curling around his groin like a deadly harness. The bobbing head beneath the sheet moved free as he sacrificed grip for swinging force and brought the butt of the bottle up and over, smashing it down onto the snake's head.

The movement caused the bottle to glance off to one side, stunning, but not stopping the reptile.

Slayton slammed the flat of his hand against the shape and bashed it three quick times against the carpet, an animal grunt escaping him each time. There was a liquid crunch, and the sheet began to darken in his hands. Slayton kept swinging and smashing until the sound was like someone striking a wet sponge, and then he fell backward, slumping against the wall in the narrow space between it and the bed, the black coils imprisoning his legs and privates slacking their pressure in death.

His hands were covered with blood, his body glazed with sweat. He lay in the corner, panting, trying to stabilize. The inky blotches on the sheet expanded and bordered into each other, forming a glowing blossom of red.

Shauna stood petrified, her arms bracketing the door frame. "Ben? *Ben!*"

"Yeah," Slayton said, voice hoarse, limply waving a hand in the air. His other hand covered his eyes. The blood, thinned by his sweat, trickled down his face. He could smell it.

Once, with Art Stannard and Gabriel Whitman in Texas, Slayton had played the game known as rattlesnake tag. The object was to grab a rattler tossed at you by someone else in the circle, grab it by the tail and swing it around, and then toss it at someone else. You had to catch it in flight. Skill determined which end of a spinning snake you might grab. The rattlers were sometimes six feet long.

The dead thing on the floor was well over twelve feet long, and twice as big around as the rattlers Slayton recalled.

He rose unsteadily, pushing the snake away. He weaved, crawled over the surface of the bed, and fell on the floor.

Shauna's paralysis broke, and she ran to help him.

"I think I'm going to be sick," he said, in a small voice.

She helped him get to his feet and led him to the bathroom. She wanted to stay as far away from the bed area as possible. She closed the door, hugging the wall as Slayton gave up his magnificent Haskell's dinner to the Washington sewer system. When she heard the sound of water running, she reopened the door. Steam was filling up the bathroom.

He turned and took her in his arms and they held onto each other for a moment. He blew out his breath finally and said, "I hope that wasn't a pet of yours, or something."

The sound she made was half laugh, half sob. She grabbed two fistfuls of his hair and kissed him.

There are no people so life-embracing as those who have faced death together. Slayton and Shauna made fervent love in the tub, drenching the entire bathroom. And then again.

At last they lay deep in steam and cloudy suds, his head buttressed against the faucet and hers at the opposite end, psychologically cleansed as well as physically drained.

"Let's get dressed and dispose of the garbage," he said in even tones, now fully under control. He tickled one of her generous nipples with his big toe, causing lazy eddies in the water. "I want to see those crates you mentioned tonight."

"How are you going to—" She looked toward the door.

"I am going to go to wherever the ice and soft drink machines are to be found in this lodge, and steal the plastic bag out of the trash can you always find there. I'm going to touch that monster out there one more time, and then pack him and the sheet out of your sight and mine. If I get my sense of humor back between now and then, I may just leave our visitor in the hotel swimming pool. Or maybe the wishing well in the lobby."

"Ben, does this mean . . . ?"

"Darlin', this has everything to do with what I was just telling you about. We'd better get started."

10

"These marks were on the crates before we ever opened them up," said Shauna. "Like they were pried open."

"But nothing's missing," said Slayton.

"Right. Now look at this. This box was ninety percent padding and fiber; there's a space in the middle where something rested—something fairly big, by the size of the box and the size of the impression left by whatever was removed. It's part of our shipment, and it was accounted for on the manifest of the *Star of Egypt*. But whatever was in here is gone." She shrugged.

The Seth-Olet exhibit, now uncrated for the most part, nevertheless required that the shipping materials be maintained almost as carefully as the artifacts themselves. It was three o'clock in the morning, and with the benediction of the Sparta men, Slayton and Shauna were mucking about in the boxes, now disconnected from the tractor trucks, adding chunks to the puzzle.

Slayton examined the box Shauna said had been pried open. It was composed of multiple layers of cardboard, slatted wood for structural rigidity, and many thicknesses of padding. It was designed to keep its hard side outward, its soft sides toward the contents.

Slayton looked at her briefly and said, "May I?" indicating the wall of the box. She nodded.

He drummed his fingers against the flat wood, sounding the material. Abruptly he stepped back, pivoting at the waist and driving the heel of his hand into the solid wood with considerable force. It cracked hollowly and collapsed inward, the outside facing apparently turning out to be only thin plywood.

"Look inside," he said.

"You didn't come all the way through," she told him.

"Yeah. But look at my arm." It was sunk into the side of the box to the elbow, yet she could not see his hand within. "Dummy facing," he said. "Where once there was padding, now there is a hidden storage area. If you casually ripped off the lid, it wouldn't give itself away, but if you knew which nails to yank out, you could slide this whole section out, like the door of an elevator—a lift—clean out the compartment, and replace it." He tapped the wood.

There was a rueful expression on Shauna's face in the semidarkness. "And nobody finds out until long after the ship docks . . ." she said, looking pained. "Not only that, but the optimum protection for the artifacts we're supposed to get from these is gone. Oh, bloody hell!"

Slayton felt like a teacher giving a familiar lecture once too often. "And since, when you're a smuggler, it never pays to put all your eggs in one basket, you employ several methods in case the cover gets pulled on one or two of them en route. Here we have a gimmicked box. But this—" He indicated the second huge crate Shauna had pointed out to him. "—is the result of a faked manifest. This says it's yours, but it isn't. And there are probably two or three more gimmicks we haven't spotted yet."

"What could take up so much room?"

"Well, the only thing truly harder than weapons to smuggle is large groups of people, and that's out. I'm thinking guns. I've seen some photos to back that up. Conversely," he added, "dope is the easiest thing in the universe to sneak in and out of countries. That people still get caught at it is a testament to their amateurishness. But guns—"

He paced around some of the other boxes, browsing, considering other angles he didn't really need, now that he had satisfied himself that the smuggling had been real—he did not expect to find leftovers hanging around.

"Guns you can get anywhere, especially in the United States. Any shmuck can buy one, even stolen military stock, automatic weapons, explosives—no trouble here. America is the land of free enterprise. You smuggle guns if you need disposable weapons in a hurry, or if you don't trust anyone outside to handle your armaments. The catch is, to smuggle guns and have it be worthwhile, you've got to smuggle a *lot* of guns." More to himself than anything, he said, "He not only got himself past us, but his goddam arsenal too."

"You know, that crate with all the straw would be the perfect thing to ship over a—" Her voice caught, just slightly. "—a big snake like that."

"King cobra," Slayton said. "Jesus. The only time I'd ever seen one of those things was on a reptile farm. They grow to be eighteen, twenty feet long, sometimes more. Which is just about twenty feet too long for my taste."

"I couldn't believe what you did back there," she said. "To think that that thing might have been on the ship with us the whole time . . ."

"Yeah," Slayton said, suddenly brightening. "Somebody had to tend to it—if only to make sure it didn't die in transit."

"Sorry," said Shauna. "Can't help you. No herpetologists that *I* know of in the bunch." Then she said, "I know a sneaky way that might help us, though."

Slayton raised his eyebrows, attentive.

"Ahmed Sadi . . . uh, is rather enamored of our own Maggie. It's her hair. If she quizzed him on this, he'd turn the work crew inside out trying to fill the bill. We might wind up with just a scapegoat, but it's more than we have at the moment."

"Good," said Slayton. "It's a start. I've got some records and things to check."

She immediately became defensive. "No. I *don't* want to crawl back into that bed and pretend to try to go to sleep, because that will be useless. And you know it."

"And *you* know we can't be much good as a team if we're spliced onto each other constantly," Slayton said, becoming stern. "I'll relocate you, get you out of that place, at least."

Shauna bit her lip. "Okay, okay." She understood, and that was a relief to Slayton.

"Tell you what," she said. "I'll ring Maggie back at the hotel. But I'm not going to tell her exactly where I've relocated. As long as I'm on time and on the job, it doesn't really matter where I stay, and I really don't have to account to anybody for my off time. This way, maybe we can have results by morning."

"Alright," Slayton said. "Let's get out of here before we uncrate something else that bites."

Shauna did not need to be convinced to leave.

Professor Gordon Willis had handled snakes.

Slayton shifted the folder on his lap. The Professor must have, he thought, if he had poked around in half the tombs his dossier suggested. An unlikely possibility, but there. Maggie Leiber had frequently been unaccounted for during the voyage, wandering around the ship, but she didn't seem the right temperament for it. Slayton's instinct pulled him toward Ahmed Sadi, but the boisterous Arab was usually highly visible—he certainly did not have time to supervise two loadings on the docks simultaneously. He *had* been one of the first to rush over following the incident with the forklift—it would have been simple to merely double back. . . .

"Let's see if I can get anyone to flinch at the word *snake*," he said to himself, knowing that that, too, was halfhearted.

Then there was still the trio of Willis's diggers—Cooke, Winslow, and Pratley. They all checked out as adventurous European knockabouts; unimaginative academic careers stopped somewhere midway, followed by a fairly predictable run of caving, mountaineering, and touring the continent with practically no support whatsoever. Their function on the tour was principally to provide a counterpoint to the stuffy technicalities of Professor Willis' speechmaking by hitting the university campus audiences *hard* with personal anecdotes and adventures. Tanned, assured, muscular, and self-confident, as well as having a legitimate claim to being worldly, they were a perfect advertisement for drumming up support and interest in Willis's endeavors.

During Slayton's primary interview, they had appeared bored but amused. They had promptly vanished into the campus milieu in order to meet their tight speech-making schedules. From the moment the *Star of Egypt* had docked, they were, for all intents and purposes, booked up.

Too bad they could not loiter around, thought Slayton, even as potential allies. They would have been the most useful—they had a profound sense of teamwork, among other things, and were virtually inseparable. "Randy little buggers," Shauna had said, with the sort of affection one reserves for wayward younger brothers. "I sometimes suspect they realized this tour would be practically a sexual smorgasboard of America—Willis did not have to do much in the way of convincing them."

The trio was essentially irrelevant to Slayton's problem. Though even his brief talk with them had been enough for him to register that these three were, in every way, apolitical European youngsters unconcerned with the power squabbles that were the stock in trade of people like Slayton, or, for that matter, Rashid Haman. Instead of shooting and point-making, they were balling their merry way through life. Slayton shook his head and added their dossier to the filtered stack.

Slayton, now alone, was acutely aware of his increasing physical need to strike back at Haman. It was pure frustration at being toyed with. He wanted to corner the elusive, damnable man, and take him on barehanded, one-on-one.

It would be easy for Hamàn to be one of the crew, any of the crew—*all* of the crew. Slayton kept running up against that particular investigative brickwall. He had to trust Ahmed Sadi, but what if he was Haman?

Slayton regarded the accumulated documents stacked on the table before him. There was Winship's material, Wilma's research, his own notes gleaned from observation and the copious details given to him by Shauna, the photos, dossiers, profiles of each member of the expedition, xeroxes—in all, a library that was doing him little direct good. In that moment, he decided that his mind would sift and retain whatever would be needed in a crunch, and henceforth it would of necessity be his hunches and instincts that would have to carry him. He had to approach this problem with the same sort of animal cunning Haman would apply—and *was* applying even now—to bedevil him.

That determined, Slayton left the papers on the table and regarded the slowly rising sun through a nearby window.

He had to start early, regardless of the fact he had gotten little sleep during the night with Shauna, the cobra, and the hunt-and-peck session aboard the truck trailers. He decided he'd better get a shave before leaving.

The grin on Ahmed Sadi's face was almost cinematically apologetic.

"We seem to have misplaced one of our men, sir," he told Slayton, as the two walked along outside the exhibit center. "Miss Dr. Leiber spoke to me this morning—ah, she is so beautiful, is she not, sir?"

Slayton nodded.

"She asked me some most peculiar questions about the handling of animals," he continued. "I mentioned that several men in my humble contingent had occasion to work for foreign collections—zoos and that sort of thing."

"And the man foremost in your mind as fitting her description has now disappeared?" Slayton felt a different kind of snake twist uncomfortably in his gut.

"Yes, Mr. Rademacher. You remember Bassam."

"The one who seemed so offended by my interview?"

"Yes sir, indeed."

This seemed even stranger to Slayton. Haman would certainly not try to draw attention to himself by being immediately hostile, and then being the first person to split when questions were asked. And then he thought: *misdirection.*

"Where would he go? He's practically a tourist, Ahmed."

"Ah, yes, sir. I think he will turn up here again soon. Unless he abandons us altogether."

In which case we've got nothing to worry about, Slayton added mentally. Maybe he'll go to work for the Bronx Zoo.

After being waved through into the exhibit area, Slayton found that the background flats had been erected, and now the area actually did look like the interior of a tomb. Two men were doing some preliminary fiddling with lighting effects and baby spots. Shauna was busy at a work table near what she had earlier described as the coffin area, brushing and inspecting what looked like a mask.

"Death mask?" said Slayton, and she looked up.

"Hardwood face," she said. "Laid over the real thing. Look, see—the eyes are made of obsidian."

He inspected the article briefly. She lowered her voice so the others in the room would not hear: "My god, Ben, you know now that it's morning, I find myself disbelieving that adventure last night . . ."

"What adventure?" said Slayton, picking up an amulet from the table.

She shook her head. "Did you find out anything?"

"No." He paused, really wishing he could tell her something positive, allay whatever demons were pestering her now. "This is a *hydrocephalus*—correct me if I'm wrong. What does it say?"

"It's a rubric from Chapter 162 of the Book of the Dead," she said, holding the amulet in both hands before her face and calling up the passage from memory. "That's the 'chapter of making heat to be under the deceased.' It reads: *O Amon, O Amon, who art in heaven, turn thy force upon the dead body of thy son and make him sound and strong in the Underworld.* You'd better be free tonight, damn you."

"Does it say that, too?" He smiled. "Depends. Maggie paid off, after a fashion. One of the workers has vanished."

"A suspect?"

"Not really."

"Well, I hope I can see you later. Did you speak to Maggie outside?"

"No, I missed her."

"If you spot her, tell her her counsel is urgently requested, in Hell's Kitchen. She's probably at the hotel, on the phone. And I *will* see you later. Careful with that stuff; all those little vials are full of acid." She said this last without even looking up.

Slayton replaced the test-tubelike container he had lifted from the table. "Acid?"

"Nitric acid, flouric acid, hydrochloric. Sometimes we need it to clean these things. Sparing dosages only. Don't get your nose too close, kind gentleman." She gave him a wry look, and he departed.

"Been to bed with her yet?" came a voice as soon as Slayton was back outside.

Still staring straight ahead, Slayton said, "Was there ever a man more misunderstood? Hello, Wilma."

"I won't quote you," she said, catching up with him and matching his pace. "But don't tell me you two haven't made a point of staying within striking distance of each other."

"I have to watch over them."

"Why?"

"Top secret," he mumbled.

"No fair." She let it die out and then said, "Those trucks, and those shipments of weapons—if they *were* weapons—have melted into the woodwork. No traces, nothing. Sorry about that."

"Both of us," said Slayton, distractedly. "I got attacked by a king cobra last night, in my bedroom."

Wilma cocked an eyebrow. "That's what you get for sleeping out on me, bastard."

"Wilma, speaking of those trucks—"

She cut him off. "You're not going to talk about it, are you!" She shook her head, incredulous.

"Not polite. You know me, the soul of tact and all that. Look—here's a man you just have to meet. Broaden your horizons." Ahmed Sadi approached them on the walk.

"Oh, boy," she said.

Ahmed was more than pleased to meet Wilma, who shot one of her *I'll return the favor someday, smartass* looks at Slayton while being TV-polite. Slayton, naturally, had immediate business that required him, regrettably, to be elsewhere. It never happened.

From across the small courtyard, somebody started shooting at them.

Three flat and very loud reports cracked and echoed off all the cement. At the sound of the first, Slayton grabbed Wilma, pushing her to the ground with himself over her—they were flat down, but needed substantial cover. Ahmed dived behind a shrub. They were all too far away from the door to the exhibit hall to make a run for it.

A hot slug skimmed off the sidewalk near Slayton, and the second blew brick chips out of the building wall behind them. He heard the third ricochet, but did not see where it went.

He did hear Ahmed scream out in pain.

11

"Stackman! Stackman, are you back there!"

Stackman was, in fact, holed up in the exhibit hall entrance, pistol drawn. "Yeah!"

"Take two guys and bear straight in on him—one down that breezeway over there, and the other on the other side," shouted Slayton. With guards headed down the breezeways, the man shooting—who Slayton now realized was across the courtyard—would have to retreat through the alley to the rear. It was the only way.

"Wilma!" Slayton yelled. "Are you—"

"Yeah, yeah," Wilma said, still on the ground, covering her ears with her hands.

Slayton was off and running. He had already determined that if he was the target, his assailant was a lousy shot. If there was any more fire, Stackman and his cohorts, now charging up the breezeways as instructed, would return fire, and that would be chaotic enough for Slayton not to worry too much about getting clipped. He ran.

With Stackman and his men right behind, Slayton caught a corner of the building and tore around it just in time to see a Levi-clad ass bounce over a chain link fence at the dead end of the alley, where the tour cars were generally parked. Slayton did not know what was beyond the fence. The mystery did not slow him down, and in seconds he was up and over the fence himself.

"That dude is long gone," said Stackman, disgusted. He motioned his men to quit running. They stared at the fence in the distance, obscured by the junk leaning against the opposite side. "Rademacher!" he called, his hands cupped over his mouth. "Jesus, *both* of them are long gone . . ."

Slayton was motioned into absolute silence by a panting Bassam, who had doubled back and, under cover, waited for Slayton to come over the fence. Obscured from the view of the Sparta men, Slayton stood with his hands slowly elevating skyward as Bassam held the big .45 on him as steadily as he was able.

Christ! thought Slayton. The bastard's so nervous that if he hiccups, he'll blow off my arm at the elbow.

"You will not be moved," Bassam said, warily.

"Right." Slayton tensed and said, "Why didn't you let anyone know you could speak English, Bassam?"

"I am only a little." That was for sure. He motioned with the pistol toward the fence.

Slayton picked it up. "Bassam, I don't think they followed me."

"To your automobile we will!" Again, instructive movements with the gun. He was extremely agitated and touchy. "You ahead of me, now." Beyond the fence there was a narrow rift between two taller buildings, and it was toward this that Bassam directed Slayton.

The passage was just several inches wider than Slayton's shoulders. Bassam was shorter, and seemed agile enough. Slayton gauged his chances as he moved ahead. From this end, the rift looked like a long, thin tunnel. It did not admit much daylight., Bassam would have the pistol aimed at his back, just a bit high.

It would take him a second to panic and shoot. He might continue to fire mechanically, but he would hesitate before that first shot, would wait to make sure that Slayton's actions deserved the shooting. That hesitation would be all the delay Slayton needed. If Bassam had intended only death, Slayton would certainly be sprawled out back by the fence now, blood coming out of six or seven holes. The man's actions broadcast uncertainty; he would hesitate. Slayton decided, and acted.

With smooth economy of motion, Slayton dropped down onto both hands and kicked straight back, hitting Bassam. He used the inertia of the kick, coming off his left hand and twisting to a stand, facing the opposite direction, as Bassam lost his balance and fell on his ass. The gun, held too tightly, went off as it swooped upward in his grip. The shell scissored madly off the close walls, bouncing from one side to the other until it was gone. Bassam had both hands on the gun and it was pointing straight up toward the sky.

Slayton wasted no time and grabbed Bassam's feet, using the motion of his backward fall against him and continuing, flipping him over. His arms flew out reflexively to brace himself against the brick walls and to avoid being somersaulted. He dropped the gun to the dirt.

Slayton jacked his arms up and Bassam did a furious three-quarter flip that landed him on his face with jarring impact. He scrabbled to his feet as Slayton kicked the pistol behind him, between his own legs.

Bassam came to his feet attempting a general open-handed grab for Slayton, but it was a move that could be seen coming for miles. Slayton deflected the smaller man's hands to either side and advanced with a salvo of flat, open-handed blows that bounced Bassam's head from one side of the rift to the other, much like the misfired bullet.

Blood spurted from Bassam's nose as he spun, arms out, against the wall to Slayton's right. Slayton angled a chop into his throat. He stiffened and his body tried to bend over, with the result he again whacked his skull, this time against the far wall. Slayton stepped up, kicked, and Bassam's breath came woofing out.

It was done, of course, but Slayton's body kept working. He slammed a fist down on the back of Bassam's neck and his body tried to crumple into a fetal position. Instantly, Slayton flipped his body over and pounced, getting a thumb onto Bassam's windpipe, totally immobilizing the Arab.

Bassam was already unconscious. Slayton almost broke the man's nose with another efficient blow before he noticed.

And then Slayton stood up, feeling a rush of something like nausea, very like the sensation that had overcome him after the incident with the cobra, only less pronounced.

At once, he realized his body was unleashing and burning those massive backups of aggression and adrenalin. His collected frustration against Rashid Haman had just bled off a huge reserve of power in a quick burst. It was like opening and slamming a door, getting a blinding burst of light from within in the quick interim. He might have gone on to kill the Arab, had he not checked himself immediately.

But now Slayton immediately bent to check Bassam's pulse and respiration. He was still alive, his autonomic nervous system pulling in his breath mechanically. The blood streaming out of his nose lagged a little in its flow. Some had trickled into his mouth and outlined his teeth in red. Slayton examined the man quickly and economically. He had a goose-egg lump bulging from the back of his skull and abrasions on his face from the rough bricks of the building wall, but there were no broken bones—in a day or two, the only souvenirs Bassam would have would be some unattractive contusions.

Slayton scooped the smaller man out of the dirt and hoisted him arm-and-leg over his shoulders, creeping sideways until they were clear of the narrow gap between the buildings.

Then he remembered the gun.

He leaned the inert form of Bassam against the building wall and dashed back. The gun was covered with dirt from the struggle. The nickel plating was nicked and scratched. As soon as Slayton picked it up he realized that it was his own .45 automatic, from the Triumph—which was still in Baltimore, of course.

A quick check of the clip revealed only the four shots had been fired. Slayton stuck the gun in his belt, collected Bassam, and headed back for the exhibit hall area.

People were clustered near the entrance, where the gunplay had disrupted everything. A police car and an ambulance were bouncing their lights off the surrounding buildings.

If it hadn't been for their fear that Ben would return on a stretcher, both Shauna and Wilma might have found the superman image of Slayton returning from the chase, his attacker softened up and draped across his shoulders almost comic. Of course, once off the ground, Wilma had captured everything with her little Minolta, and she stepped forward now to snap a shot of Slayton, carrying Bassam.

"Gotcha, hero," she said.

"Jesus Christ, Wilma!" he began, and then she hurried forward and said, out of earshot of the group, "Don't worry, don't worry, your mug isn't going to grace *our* pages. Your anonymity is secure. This is for my scrapbook."

"I'll bet," he said, rolling his eyes and dumping Bassam onto a stretcher rolled up by two paramedics. He walked immediately over to the ambulance unit, peered in, and saw Ahmed Sadi growling at the men attempting to minister to his arm.

"Goddam stupid incompetent camel-shit idiot," he screamed. "You're breaking my bleeding arm!"

"The bleeding is *from* your arm, which is already broken," murmured the medic, in a tone which suggested he was treating just the disembodied limb, and not the Arab attached to it.

Slayton flashed his credentials brief. It had become a habit around police to save arguing time. "Doc—what's the story with him?"

Still not looking up from his work, his hands coated with Ahmed's blood, the man said, "I am not a doctor. Doctors can diagnose and give injections. They also don't have to put up with as much horseshit as I'm putting up with now." He leaned across the berth, bracing Ahmed's unwounded arm, suddenly speaking with his nose an inch away from the Arab's. "Listen, you. Any more thrashing and you're gonna mess up this art work I did on your arm. Cuss me to the dogs and back, my man, but do it in Arabic or I'll break your fucking jaw. Got it?"

Ahmed, just as suddenly, became quite calm. "I like you," he said in a tone that abruptly denied the pain he was suffering.

"Okay," the medic said, finishing with the bleeding arm. Then he ducked his way out of the med unit, towelling his hands and arms. "Bullet did some real mean damage," he said to Slayton. "You know what kind of slug it was? You a cop?"

Slayton grimaced. He knew too well. He kept the .45 as a pay-or-play last resort, with a close-quarters blow-away in mind. It was not a long range weapon. The slugs had been carefully scooped out and crosshatched. Had Bassam been closer, Ahmed's entire arm would have disappeared at the shoulder.

"Got another one for your services," he said, indicating Bassam.

"He shot, too? Looks like someone thought he was a steak and tried to tenderize him."

"He just needs first aid," Slayton said, as he saw the cops approaching. He'd have to field them, as well.

He remanded custody of Bassam to the cops but left out the details of the gun, which he had ditched in his car on the way back.

"Isolation," he said, pointing in the cop's face. "He talks to nobody but me and an interpreter, maybe. This is government business."

The cop, who did not wish to complicate his day, indicated that it was no problem, and within half an hour everyone had lost their chance at fame.

"I can see you're going to be in good hands," Wilma said snidely. "I have to go—you know—" She gestured toward her camera and tape recorder.

Slayton put out a cautionary hand. "Wilma, go slow, okay? You know my usual entreaties, and they all apply right now." She nodded, against her news judgment. "That's pretty damn good," he continued. "Your grace under fire, I mean."

"What you *mean,*" she said pointedly, "is that it was good for a *girl,* right? Save the butter for the bedroom, Ben. Maybe I'll see you *later.*" She stalked off.

He made a helpless gesture, but she was gone. He already knew by heart the argument they would move through later.

"It's safe to assume, I suppose, that somewhere in there is a loving human being," came Shauna's voice from behind him.

"Now who's sounding competitive and threatened?" Slayton said, spinning on her. "Ah, god . . . don't start, Shauna, okay? Suddenly I'm getting a real pisser of a headache."

"Fair enough," she said. "Willis won't care what all the hysteria was about, but Maggie will want to know. What should I tell her?"

"No, I'll deal with it," he said.

"Brave lady," she said, looking off in the direction Wilma had gone. "She almost got blown away."

"Yeah," Slayton said, leading Shauna back toward the exhibit hall. "Didn't we all?" His mind was racing furiously through bits and pieces of detail, trying to move, then coalesce into some shape, no matter how undefined.

"I suppose now that you've got him—" Shauna hesitated. "No, that's not right. I was going to say now that you've got him, you're done and you'll be leaving, and wait for you to snap at it. That's not fair." They had stopped in the vestibule of the building. "It's not true, either."

"Sounds like you've done the entire conversation in advance," Slayton said. He took up both of her hands. "Look. Now's not the time, at any rate. Let's get the opening out of the way—you know how full my hands are going to be in about an hour?"

Her face was fraught with indecision. "Yes, yes . . . but I just . . . last night and now this . . . to think that that was the man who was responsible, and now that you're done with your—your *job,* you'll just—"

"Shh!" went Slayton, loudly. It startled her, and she stopped.

"What?" she said, unconsciously adopting a stage whisper.

"SHH!" Slayton's eyes bulged with an almost comic anger. Her eyes darted from side to side, seeking potential danger.

"SHH!" he went again, and this time she smiled. "Are you finished?" he said.

Shauna covered her eyes, and then laughed. When she came out from behind the hand her eyes were wet, but she could not keep the smile off her face. "Yes. Okay, I tried to do my speech." She snickered.

"And you blew it," Slayton said. "Hold still." He took her face in his hands and kissed her, long and completely. "Don't worry about that little terrorist subplot over there. I will see you later, regardless of him."

"Alright."

They parted, to take care of separate business.

Slayton did not know exactly what, but something had stopped him from telling Shauna Ramsey that Bassam could not, by any stretch of the imagination, be a terrorist, let alone Rashid Haman. Or that Ahmed was also out, by virtue of the week he would now spend in the hospital. Something had warned him away from telling her.

12

"The results of the interrogations certainly seem odd to me," Winship said, as he gazed benignly out a floor-to-ceiling window, arms behind his back.

"How so, sir?" Slayton was standing near the desk.

"We should be able to consider this case closed—at least, in terms of safety to the Seth-Olet tour. You deny that this fellow Bassman—"

"Bassam," said Slayton. "He's Egyptian."

"There, you see? He makes you early on in the tour and tries to eliminate you first chance he gets. If he had pegged you in front of the exhibit hall, it certainly would have gotten the opening cancelled. How to get at the President then? How to disrupt the tour in a propaganda-effective fashion?"

"Sir—"

"Diversionary tactic, I say. We were waiting for him to make a move, so he made a purely gratuitous one and got caught."

"Sir, there's no way Bassam could be Rashid Haman, if only on the basis of gutlessness. Bassam has no stomach for killing. Haman likes it."

"I'm tempted, you know, to dismiss this along with the rest," said Winship, turning now. "It would be a great relief if Haman turned out to be a much more disappointing specimen than we suspected—"

"—if for no other reason than it took me down a few notches," said Slayton.

"You must admit that you've been doing some pretty broad propagandizing for the man, yourself," Winship said academically. "But I'm inclined to agree with you. Rashid Haman wouldn't blow a setup as perfect as the President and the exhibit together by getting apprehended on the day prior to the opening of the exhibit itself."

"Unless his job was already done. Yes, sir—I thought of that, too."

"This man claims that he knows nothing of the Arab terrorists. That, in fact, he fled Egypt to get away from that particular brouhaha. He told us that he was informed that you were an undercover agent for Immigration, and that it was your job to apprehend him by force and deport him to Egypt, since it turns out he has entered the country illegally. He took the place and identity of one of the crew members—his brother. His name is really Nadim."

"I'd buy everything except the obvious setup—that I was supposed to roust him. That's obviously designed to get me personally."

"So the question is: Who primed Bassam?"

"He claims the gun was left for him along with a note, in Arabic, in his room. Since he was already running scared," Slayton said, thinking of Bassam's attitude during his questioning, "it only took that much to set him off. He was extremely highstrung, agitated, working on the paranoia of getting caught throughout the whole voyage and setup."

"Do you think he is the one who attacked you with the forklift in the warehouse?" asked Winship, point-blank.

"No sir." Slayton considered that. "Possible, yes, but not likely. Why wait so long, when I was around all the time, to try again if he was going to kill me anyway? The expedient thing would have been to get rid of me right away."

"What about that somewhat fanciful adventure you related about the—that snake coming after you in your bedroom?"

"I think Bassam handled the snake. Whether he planted it, I don't know. Either way, it would mean he was in on this last night, which means he's lying about the note."

Slayton also had a collection of theories about Rashid Haman that he was now keeping strictly to himself. The official opening of the Seth-Olet exhibit was less than twenty-four hours away, which meant, in Haman terms, now was the time to pour on the pressure, now was the time for resolution, the point at which Slayton would either win or lose the game.

He understood Bassam's role only too well. He played the part of sacrificial lamb. In all probability, the man had been cajoled into actions by threats from Haman directly. Bassam knew the horrible potential penalties for exposing Haman—and at any rate, there was no way they'd get him to crack by tomorrow afternoon. Haman was timing things with his usual care.

Bassam had been thrown to the wolves by Haman as a steam valve, to sate the frustrations of Slayton and others anxious to collar someone, anyone other than Haman. It was time purchased.

What it meant to Slayton, in a nutshell, was that he was getting close enough to the truth to make Haman uncomfortable.

"Make sure the exhibit is secure by tomorrow morning," said Winship. "Do that, and you're free to pursue your own course of investigation. God knows we'll never get anywhere this way."

"It won't be any trouble to hold Bassam in custody for the immigration rap, will it?"

Winship shook his head, as though bothered with a triviality.

"Good," said Slayton. "Slap a guard or two on his ward. Haman will probably try to kill him."

"What about that other fellow?"

"Ahmed? He was a chief suspect until this mess." The more Slayton thought about Ahmed's place in the game, the more he considered the brash play with Bassam a mistake on the part of Rashid Haman. The prime suspect had been accidentally eliminated, a plate of armor had been removed. The idea that it was a goof appealed to Slayton. It made Haman less superhuman.

"I think he's innocent. But if I may recommend it, sir—"

"Guards for him, too?"

"We should only need them for a day or so," Slayton countered.

"What about that reporter who was there during the shooting?" said Winship, seemingly endorsing the extra guards for Ahmed in passing.

"We've got a very tentative press blackout on this until tomorrow, sir. The items on the Seth-Olet tour itself don't mention the Department, or any of the details relating to Rashid Haman."

"Do you know the reporter personally?"

"Ah—yes sir. Ms. Wilma Christian."

A great volume of information seemed to pass between Slayton and Winship in one nuclear flash of telepathy. Winship moved his head from side to side, slowly, like a bronze statue coming to life, and then his focus returned to the desk to search for the pipe.

"Improper channels, Slayton," he said at last.

Slayton stifled a grin in his own self-interest. "Improper, sir?"

"Unreliable." The word hinted that Winship might prefer more concrete methods of assuring cooperation from the press—like leg irons and mouth-blocks. "You have to go," he said, dismissing the topic of Wilma Christian as well.

The drive back to the domain of Seth-Olet was a short one for Slayton, not nearly time-consuming enough to reconcile the things his mind did not really want to consider.

Shauna had been on tap for the incident with the cobra. It could all have been a bizarre act of some kind.

Shauna was the one who started the wheels in motion—the inquiry on the cobra—that caused the fiasco with Bassam.

Shauna had been in the Triumph. Somehow the gun had gotten from the car—once she knew he kept one, it was easy to assume he hid it in his government-issue vehicle as well—to Bassam's room.

Shauna seemed determined to bowl him over with affection when he started asking questions. She had been the one who demonstrated—or rather, let Slayton demonstrate for himself—the gimmicked crates. My god, she could have had him in the back of the truck! But it was common practice for victors to show the defeated subjects just how they had been duped, therefore defeated, once the method could not harm anybody. It was a distasteful form of gloating.

Shauna had, in all probability, witnessed the entire shooting incident from a window of the exhibit hall. With a stop watch, perhaps?

And she had—if this line of logic was to be productive at all—infiltrated the enemy camp in the best way possible. She was sleeping with Ben Slayton.

Maggie Leiber had called Shauna the "dragon lady." She had told Slayton things in conversational passing that hinted at a sort of gruesome composure. Odd for someone with Shauna's outward persona—wasn't it Shauna herself who had brought up multiple personae and carped on the equality of females in the Egyptian god-hierarchy?

"Surely you've noticed how predatory this job has made her," Maggie had told him.

Circumstantial evidence rather than logic told him that Shauna Ramsey was a threat; his instinct felt extremely "warm." Another sensation, twisting with sadistic glee in his gut, said she could not possibly be anything as dangerous as a Rashid Haman—a primal and outmoded feeling, it was true, but jammed in the back of Slayton's mind nevertheless—a woman could not possibly accomplish the feats attributed to Haman.

But there was just enough doubt.

There was also something like eighteen hours left.

Maggie Leiber was just a little bit surprised at Slayton's strange offer.

"I hope your schedule is just hectic enough, Doctor, that I might woo you away for a brief cruise of the Potomac. Automobile, of course—I loaned my canoe to some Cherokee tourists who made me an offer I couldn't refuse. So if you turn me down now, I'll be crushed. Please come. I have to talk to you, and I promise to have you back before they notice you've been kidnapped."

She was amused by the whole presentation. "High and dry and *sans* canoe. Good god, it would be an act of samaritanism. Which way to your car?"

Her enthusiasm dulled somewhat when Slayton rather aggressively turned the topic of conversation over to Shauna.

"What I meant when I spoke to you before," she said, "was that Shauna's sexual forthrightness seemed to be in direct contradiction to her personality. I don't pretend to be a Sunday-supplement shrink, Ben, but who would believe me if I told them that that creature, broadcasting sexual messages on every possible wave band when you, for example, come into the room, is really as secretive as a monk with a vow of silence? I suppose that's an unlikely mix of metaphors, but what the hell."

"Just to stay Biblical," he said, and smiled. "What kind of secrecy? Maggie, believe me please, because we're running out of time, it's important. Everything's important."

"Well, she apparently knows people in Washington, or somewhere here, because she keeps shooing me out of her room in order to make phone calls. Yesterday, for no reason, she lugged a small carton of artifacts home with her, ostensibly to clean them up. But Ben, the guards would have seizures if they'd known she had removed items from the hall. We all trust her, of course, but why take them back to clean them when that could be done here? That's the kind of strange I mean."

Slayton felt a gnawing sense of urgency, but his diplomatic instincts won out, forcing him to slow down and not bulldog Maggie. It would be a vast mistake to do things too fast just because of the time limit he felt looming ahead of him.

"I'll bet you thought I was trying to coerce you away from ancient Egypt for a drink or something."

"Well—" she said, drawing the word out. "I'll admit it crossed my mind. But that's really the sort of thing that cries out to have more time invested in it, doesn't it? I wouldn't want to be the component of what we might, in our less lucid moments, call a 'quickie.' "

"No indeed," he said, unconsciously mimicking her speech pattern. "But there's booze if you'd care to make a libation to the very near future."

Her direct, gray eyes brightened. "Oh, you're a saint! Where?" She was looking around the interior of the car with something like childish joy, a new expression to Slayton.

"Glove box," he said.

"Most people in America call it a 'compartment,' " she said, reaching in and drawing out a silver flask that had been a Christmas gift to Slayton from Wilma Christian a few seasons back.

"Ahmed got me started on flasks," he fibbed.

She sniffed. "Scotch. Thank god." She took a dignified little pull and then wiped her lips, passing the flask across. They hit a stop light as Slayton took a hit, and Maggie dissolved into gales of laughter at the haughty indignity evinced by two elderly ladies in the VW that had pulled up alongside them. When Slayton heard their chatter about the evils of combining the bottle and the wheel, he laughed, too.

"If we were on the opposite side I'd moon them," Maggie said in a mischievously quiet voice.

"I'll pull up and pass if you want," he offered quickly.

"No, kind sir, I dare not. It would too quickly evoke those long-gone college days. Fancy's passed, anyway." She took another short sip and stowed the flask, crossing her legs in the cramped foot well and watching the road. "It's three o'clock," she said.

"Oops, pumpkin time. I may break a few local laws, but I'll get you back. They let us go any speed we want in the United States, you know." He pulled ahead and maneuvered to make the best legal time back to the exhibit hall. "And I've got some things to check up on as well."

"Don't worry, you may get to see it later," she said.

"What's that?" he said, slightly turning his head.

She watched the road. "Nothing."

13

Even if Slayton had lacked a key to Shauna's new hotel room, getting one from the desk would have been simplicity itself—he had checked her in. And lacking any kind of key, his talented fingers could do away with the standard hotel-issue deadbolts in something under fifteen seconds. There was no breaking as such involved on his part—only entering.

Soon the cold, sweaty second wherein his body verified that the room was empty had passed. There was always that residual tingle of getting caught in the act. But he was alone, and set about a task which he found both objectionable, yet necessary.

The first thing he ascertained was, despite Maggie's description, there was no carton of *objets d'art* skimmed from the Seth-Olet shipment—merely one figurine, one of those Shauna had described as *Ushabtiu* figures. This one was in the likeness of Rameses VI.

He hit the closets, the toilet tank, the undersides of the drawers, and the standard search spread, taking up a neat five minutes in general looking. He sounded the mattress on the bed and went through every pocket on every article of clothing he could find. As best he could, he verified the contents of the glass and plastic medicine vials in the bathroom and near the bed.

A glass pill bottle, labeled Dexedrine, was not what it claimed to be. It was filled with liquid.

Slayton recognized fluoric acid, which he avoided inhaling, since fluorine, its base element, was normally a toxic gas. Beside the bottle on the night table was one of Shauna's Egyptology references.

Something extremely vague nagged at Slayton from his sketchy research. Wasting time was not advisable, but he took a moment to sit on the bed and go to the book, looking up Rameses VI, forcing himself not to rush.

Rameses VI dated from the 20th Dynasty. The Seth-Olet material, as he had observed earlier, had come out of a *mastăba,* a truncated, oblong form of tomb. *Mastăbas* were pre-Dynastic; Rameses VI was 20th Dynasty. He was as out of place, temporally, as a knight in armor at a bus stop in Harlem.

Slayton picked up the figure. Sure, *mastăbas* were pre-Dynastic. That didn't mean they were not used in later eras. They just did not have that much flash. . . . He had lifted the figure, which was composed of a rudimentary porcelain, and almost immediately noticed that the weight was wrong. He flipped it over. The porcelain did not look ancient or restored, but seemed to be of a much more recent vintage—the kind tourists were gulled with in Tangier Harbor. The figure seemed hollow, but the base was solid and smooth.

From the bathroom, he retrieved a glass vitamin pill bottle with a thick bottom and used it to rap sharply on the base of the figurine. The noise of contact seemed overly loud in the funereal quiet of the room.

At once, there was a yielding crack. Slayton rapped again, and hairline cracks webbed out, dividing the base into triangular chunks which held fast. He used a thin penknife blade to peel the chunks up. They were very thin.

Rameses VI was stuffed up the middle with white putty. Slayton prodded it with his finger. Like a long-distance phone connection finally clicking and clunking home, the relays and references in his head fell into place.

The IRA had often used bombs designed with homemade fluoric acid fuses. You cracked a component of the device, and the time to detonation could roughly be determined by the hardiness of whatever the acid had to eat through. Plastique and fluoric acid worked nicely. Slayton was holding at least half a pound of plastique in his hand.

"Jesus Christ." He sat staring at the figurine, contemplating the implications of all he had unearthed, for a moment too long.

There was the sound of people in the outside corridor, and the racheting of a key in the door to the connecting room of the suite. At the first noise, Slayton was on his feet. By the time the door in the next room swung open, the rickrack was all back in place, visually undisturbed.

Strike one: The only door out of the bedroom was into the next room. Strike two: The suite was ten stories up with no balcony and no ledge; the bed was too small to belly under; and the closets were too damned obvious and open.

Silently, Slayton padded into the bathroom, stood in the bathtub, and quietly drew the curtain to at least partially hide himself.

He overheard several voices, but distance made it hard to distinguish numbers or personalities. Two minutes crept past and not once in that time did he hear Shauna's voice. If she was giving orders or supervising, she would have spoken by that time.

Sweat beads began to crawl from Slayton's scalp to his collar. There were men's voices—two separate ones, perhaps three. Maybe more. They were speaking in English. Slayton had, somewhat unfairly, expected Arabic.

"—wants to corner the—"

"—took a lot of balls to just walk past—"

Rough laughter, followed by several men talking at once. Then: "—might be right."

Very clearly: "Better take a look around to make sure."

In the shower, Slayton's heart thudded harder, the blood rushing into his ears and making the utter silence seem like the roar of a waterfall.

In the other room the men were moving about. Quick mental fill-ins told Slayton that if it had been their intention to intercept him—or someone—at the room, then they would have to check to see if there was any evidence of tampering with the objects in the suite. Now they had stopped talking and started looking.

Could it be Cooke, Winslow, and Pratley? The diggers? They all spoke English, but stilted by predominantly Scandinavian flavorings. It could be just the muffled uncertainty of the eavesdropping, but Slayton was somehow sure that it was not those three.

If it had been, he might have been able to bluff his way out, lie on the bed or something, and let the inferences fall where they might. They all would have laughed heartily, and Slayton would have been able to depart intact.

The absence of conversation from the connecting room, the silent determination of the now-searching team, seemed to eliminate that potential right away. Slayton's fist curled around the vitamin pill bottle, holding it immobile so that its contents did not rattle.

They had moved into the bedroom. One would lift up the Rameses VI *Ushabtiu* figure and see the white dust it would inevitably deposit on the dresser's surface. Then he would look underneath and see the cracks of inspection.

"This looks like it's broken, or like somebody set it down real hard."

"Just her stuff; closets are okay." A deeper voice.

"Shut up." Bronx accent. "Check in there."

The muscles in Slayton's back bunched together. He set his jaw, poising for a strike (just like the cobra, an imp gibbered in the back of his mind) as the bathroom light clicked on. Shoe leather tapped an echo out of the floor.

The shower curtain was jerked casually back.

Slayton saw the man's eyes go wide as he drove the heel of the pill bottle into his face, putting everything behind it. The bottle shattered into thick shards as Slayton felt the nose and upper teeth break beneath his hand. The man stumbled backward, flailing, and his right fist took out the bathroom mirror. The roar of splintering glass was incredible; the shattering noises reverberated back on themselves endlessly. He fell, slapping the wall for balance, hitting the door jamb, sliding down and turning off the light just as Slayton heard *jesus fucking christ* from the room outside.

As the first man fell, Slayton's hands sought quickly for a pistol, but there seemed to be none. Before the man could slump completely to the floor, Slayton grabbed him by the armpits and heaved, his feet crunching on the broken plating of the big mirror. He lifted the man up before him, lagged back for half a beat, and then charged out the bathroom door.

He collided with the second man standing in the doorway.

It was more a time-buying maneuver than anything. Slayton pistoned his legs, and drove the second man, with the unconscious attacker sandwiched between, into the far wall. To his immediate left was a third man that needed dealing with, while the second rebounded. He slammed into the wall, arms swanning out, and Slayton pivoted. The man with the staved-in face crumpled in a tumble of rubberlike arms and legs to the shag carpet.

The third man was pulling a gun out of his windbreaker. It was still too far for a direct strike, so Slayton danced around into a sweep kick. The pistol made it out, but could not be aimed in time for the man to avoid the kick turning his stomach inside out, and as he tried to dodge, his gun hand went wild. Slayton spun and stepped once more, pegging the man's wrist with his toes, and the pistol somersaulted toward the connecting door.

He came out of the spin into a solid right cross that connected low, but snapped Windbreaker's head around like a top on a string. Number Two bounced off the wall and headed for the gun on the floor. They were too far apart; Slayton had to close up the distance between them.

He raced the man toward the gun and they both halted with it between them on the floor. Number Two instantly assumed a primary offensive posture and tried to drive Slayton back with a flurry of quick jabs. Slayton countered with a *savate* kick that changed direction after the man shot down an arm-deflection for it. Instead, Slayton kicked the pistol into the bathroom, and as the man's eyes unwillingly followed it, he delivered a solid throat chop.

There was only time for one blow before Windbreaker grabbed him from behind. Slayton anticipated the meaty paw clamping down on his shoulder, but before he could shift weight into an easy throw, Windbreaker brought home a devastating shot deep into Slayton's left kidney. He felt his legs instantly trying to give way, and botched the throw, sprawling Windbreaker on the carpet beside him instead of in front of him, on top of Number Two.

Windbreaker grabbed Slayton's leg, stealing his balance as Number Two pile-drived into him. He felt his shoulderblades smash onto the soft carpeting and tried to roll backward, but Number Two still had hold of him, bearing down from above.

Slayton twisted and planted his other foot in the man's face. The force lifted the man's feet from the floor and he jack-knifed back, flailing and crashing down.

Windbreaker, the biggest and thickest of the three, rolled and tried to get a claw grip on Slayton's throat before he could move to stand. He batted the meaty fingers away and rolled hard, coming to hands and knees.

Number Two saw it and dived, trying to keep Slayton prone. Slayton braced the flying man and boosted him over-head to land on the wide dresser. It, and all of its contents, avalanched to the floor as the man's wildly grabbing hands sought purchase. He still was not out.

Windbreaker plowed into Slayton from the side. Together the two men weighed over four hundred pounds, and their impact with the divider door bent it back beyond where it was designed to go, blowing the thin masonite apart like a dry graham cracker.

They both rolled away from the door, rebounding, but Slayton managed to end up on one knee, and was able to drive his right elbow straight back into Windbreaker's mouth. He went "*gugh!*" and his grab never hooked on.

Slayton turned and looked up just in time to see the Rameses VI figurine, throttled in both of Number Two's hands, coming down with the speed of a runaway comet in the conclusion of a long arc that must have begun somewhere around the small of the man's back.

Strike three . . .

Slayton's whole universe exploded laterally outward in a shower of hot white sparks, lightning against the blackness of his inner eyelids. His entire body went deaf, blind, and numb. The sparks elongated and slowed, moving farther and farther out, like air bubbles in thick, opaque syrup. He did not know he was falling, nor did he feel the relative lack of violence with which he was introduced to the carpet.

With only a handful of hours left, Ben Slayton was quits.

14

"I suppose it's just destiny that everything should blast off on its merry way to screaming hell less than a day before the bloody opening, with a million things undone and the most reliable of workers scampering off to do god knows what with who knows who and I wind up doing everything myself, as usual, I say as bloody *usual,* and why are you standing there staring at me as though I'm a full-moon case. Are you deaf or dumb, woman, speak up, *speak up* and for christ's sake tell me something encouraging or I shall certainly scream!"

Veins stood out in relief on Professor Willis' flushed face. Maggie Leiber was certain he was, at any moment, going to hurl a priceless artifact across the room and watch it explode into useless—and worthless—fragments. In some cases, semi-decayed or aged pieces had to be reassembled, like puzzles. For it to get broken all over again seemed like a farcical waste of everyone's time.

"Where's Rademacher?" he demanded. "I want to speak with him first!"

"That's just the trouble, Gordie," Maggie said, trying to calm the steaming man down. "Nobody seems to know where he's got to. I'm sure he'll be back."

"Why did Shauna leave without telling anyone—oh, god, all these smaller pieces need to be checked off and set up." Willis made a desultory motion toward the work scattered over the table. His heart was not really in it.

Maggie could only shrug again, but she strove to make the

gesture as sympathetic as possible. She found Willis' pique funny in a sort of silent-movie-comedy way—the scientist stereotype flying into a burlesque of rage.

"And the crew chief—shot by one of his own bloody men! What happened to the security we were supposed to get from—" He nearly spluttered, considering the Sparta men. "—from *those* incompetents!"

It was impossible for Maggie to explain to Willis just what was *really* going on. It would not have been relevant to his eye no matter what the excuse; all that he could understand or care about was the disruption, or complication, at least, of the opening presentation. Smoothing such ruffled feathers was a stock-in-trade for Maggie—she was accustomed to manipulating events back onto the track with minimum fuss. Willis was almost unreasonably angry. Therefore, logic dictated to her, simple, superficial curatives would not get him back to work. He could be satisfied only by events beyond the current realm of probability.

So, she lied.

"Professor, I'll go right now and round up Shauna and find Mr. Rademacher. The crew is operating practically by reflex. I don't feel any pressing need to watchdog them this close to the opening of the tour. And you've got to get those stage-fright jitters out of your system a bit, if I may be so bold."

He was not expecting something like that. "Stage fright?" he said. "Nonsense. Never had it in my life. What are you talking about?"

"You might not acknowledge it by that name, but I'd guess you're more nervous than you'd care to admit about facing the President of the United States and his august minions tomorrow. I'd think you've been devoting too much of your time to the preparations on the exhibit—and not enough time on your speech. Hm?"

Maggie knew what she was saying; she was invoking the hallowed deity of academic respectability. All at once, Professor Willis would become a high-visibility figure, exposed to national television and newspaper coverage, and so expected to be a personality as well. He must consider not accurate dating and ancient burial procedures but, to him, the nebulous and fearsome prospect of stage presence. At ease before an audience of peers, he now must regear with the common tourist in mind.

"It's making you reactionary and snappish," she said, shifting gears and appealing directly to his sense of intellect, now. "Just cool it; sit and do nothing for a minute. A minute won't disrupt anything." She placed her hands on his shoulders and gently impelled him down. He slid easily into the metal folding chair directly behind him.

Calm rationality seemed to flow over his face in a wave. "You're right, Maggie, damn you, you're always right. Do you know what bothers me about all this?" He indicated the room, now a convoluted reproduction of the tomb of an obscure Egyptian general named Seth-Olet. "It sounds silly when I say it this way, but in a word, it's accessibility. I feel so steeped in my own speciality that it's a singularly futile proposition to try to make it palatable to laymen on a level that would satisfy us both. It would either disappoint me, or confound the public."

"That's not true," she said. "What about Mr. Rademacher? He surprised you."

His tone was flat. "Do you suppose Mr. Rademacher is a representative example of the people who will partake of this exhibit, Maggie?"

"Touché," she said. To say she thought he was would sound too glib, as though she were too anxious to get Willis back to normal. "Well, I think he's an exception, and he seems to impress you, at any rate. How about this—when you imagine the people to whom you'll be speaking, why not picture him and address them as though you were speaking directly to him? Start a trend by not talking down to your audience. They may not be as dense as you fear."

Willis smiled, apparently relieved. "It's novel, you have to give it that. Yes." He stood up and rubbed his hands together. "Get Shauna in here as soon as you find her. I do so hope she's not checked into some scenic Washington hotel with Mr. Rademacher. There'll be time enough to waste *after* we try to impress the entire country."

Maggie smiled, bemused. Mentions of sex, even oblique ones, were so far outside the Professor's normal retinue that the abrupt mention now seemed calculated to startle her. It did.

It also amused her in a more personal way, since she was certain the man who called himself Ben Rademacher could not possibly be shacked up in a hotel with Shauna Ramsey.

Hamilton Winship glared at the digital clock on the desk, wondering where in hell Ben Slayton could be, and fathoming reasons for the failure of his check-in call to come through on schedule—reasons that, he hoped, could be utilized to get Slayton to be just a bit more punctual in the future. The man just did not have enough respect, or fear, wherever authority was concerned.

On the other hand, he thought, Ben Slayton, for all his unorthodox procedures, was infinitely preferable to the programmed personalities of the gray-suited Secret Service agents who stood on a perfect crescent across from him. The faceless gray hoarde, Slayton would call them. He would not have been far wrong. The Secret Service men were singularly humorless.

Specifically, the function of these men was the protection of the President. To Winship, their attendant functions seemed mere niceties, or elaborations on their basic purpose. Of course they served as guards—or walking bullet shields—for the President's family as well, plus the Vice President, his family, and anyone else the Chief Executive cared to designate as worthy of protection. But grouped together in the sights of a psycho with a burp gun, Winship thought, there was no doubt as to who the Secret Service men would jump to the protection of first, not since that little media incident in 1963.

The men fanned out before him on the opposite side of the desk were assigned to duty relating to the safety of the President during the opening of the Seth-Olet tour, and Winship had planned on Slayton's briefing support. Now, without Slayton handling the details, he would have to wing it.

"Before you is a map of the building itself, with the layout of the exhibit components outlined in blue. The only doors you must concern yourselves with are indicated in red. The others will be locked, and will not count as useable accesses." Their attention was dutifully riveted on the tripod stand which featured the maps and diagrams.

Winship plowed ahead. "Television cameras will be placed

here and here," he said, tapping the blueprint. "Seats here. Your stations are indicated, but I want to make a few points about mobility. You are, of course, to be as unobtrusive as possible, but especially careful in this case because of the cameras—this is not your usual press conference or soapbox situation. There is the possibility that the TV crews may try to make a big deal out of the security after we screen them—media people never like being searched. We must press home the urgency of this without being anything they might interpret as oppressive.

"We are the only ones who must be aware of the possibility that Rashid Haman may attempt to infiltrate himself into the scenario. We must be prepared to act before anything is allowed to even *begin* to happen. To this end I've had Ben Slayton micro-comb the components of the exhibit itself. This is entirely separate from the screening you men will perform tomorrow morning. I will, of course, be in the audience during the presentation. Mr. Slayton may not. The one thing I must emphasize is that, should he appear suddenly, or perform actions that may seem confusing or threatening to any of you men—" He broke off in order to fix the men with his eyes, to punch home what he knew to be a crucial point. "—you must *in no way interfere* with Ben Slayton. Regardless of what he does. He has worked on this case exclusively for the past week. His actions—or whatever—may mean the difference between mayhem and stability. If he gives orders, you are to follow them. If he knocks any of you on your ass, you're to hug the floor. If he is hampered in any way from performing tasks which may close up the Rashid Haman file—and believe me, gentlemen, if there is to be a climax to this little passion play it will come with the opening of the exhibit, if not before—then I shall personally assign the offender to an Icelandic coding post. Ben Slayton has my utmost trust. He knows more about the case than anyone. And the President has already advised me that a delay or rescheduling is impossible. He will not, and I quote him directly, be intimidated by terrorists. So, the boundaries of your jobs are fairly well set. Questions?"

The line was military and unmoving. Winship felt he had done his best to get the point across in a way that was urgent without seeming superfluous.

"Mr. Slayton was, as you know, due to attend this briefing," he added. "He is still exclusively involved in the case and could not attend. Each of you men will review your individual assignments with me tomorrow morning. That's all."

He waved the men out of the office. His eyes fixed on the closing door, and then he turned back to the window, to observe Washington.

"And if Mr. Slayton has gotten himself killed," he said to the empty room, "we shift to plan B. But God help us all if we have to."

Shauna Ramsey stood amid the wreckage of her hotel suite, fighting to convince the police officers flanking her that she was dealing with a simple case of breaking and entering. Or more properly, entering and breaking, taking into account the junkyard through which she and the investigating officers had sifted, discovering nothing had been removed from the rooms. The display told her—though she neglected to mention this to the police—that Benjamin Slayton, *nee* Rademacher, was somehow involved.

And the knowledge, along with the impression that Ben was either injured or dead as a result of the freewheeling wreckage before her, was making her slightly sick.

The hotel manager, an effete type in a sky-blue leisure suit, was making a show for the police of effortlessly transferring Shauna to a fresh room, neglecting to ask her whether this was, in fact, what she desired. The taller of the two officers was devoting his attention almost exclusively to the deep V of Shauna's blouse and the suggested delights bound within, or trying valiantly to peer up the slit in her skirt as she bent to straighten or retrieve her possessions from the floor.

Far worse, his partner was handling the entire affair with the air of someone who has far better things to do than deal with "hysterical females." He sighed a lot, did his best to appear exasperated, and generally hinted that his time was being squandered.

Shauna wanted very much to see Ben Slayton alive and intact, and the indifferent behavior to which she was being subjected began to grate on her nerves.

"Look, ma'am, there's really not a whole lot that the department can do for you until we get down and file and produce suspects and that sorta thing. If you ask me, I think what we got here is just a simple case of vandalism. Teenagers, you know? Tourists are easy marks for 'em."

She wheeled and spoke with a slow menace that pulsed from her like the heat from a redly glowing coal. "Pay attention to me, because I'm only going to say this once. Watch my lips instead of my chest and you might understand." Her accent became more pronounced as her anger rose—an international trait richly exemplified. "I am not a tourist. I am a guest in your country. I am not a 'ma'am.' I hold degrees you probably never would have heard of even if you had stayed in school past the sixth grade, which I severely doubt." She stabbed a finger in the cop's direction, and he recoiled.

"You and your incompetent bully-boy friend have wasted almost an hour of my time. It is clear that between the pair of you, you anticipate taking no action save to embarrass me with your stupidity and your drooling sidelong glances. I did not request you—this man did." She motioned toward the manager, whose head came bobbing up like an Irish setter on-scent. "Deal with him. You offend me." She stepped over the broken remains of the divider door and stalked from the room.

Unfortunately, vindicating herself in this manner did nothing to ease her anxiety concerning Slayton. And if she did not get back to the exhibit hall, and back to preparations for the opening, soon, Willis would crucify her. Her chance to prove herself the asset to the tour that Maggie had always suggested she might be would be neatly blown.

There was no place for her to look for him. The questions flooded in on her, unbidden, and she found herself alone. Foremost among the things etching her curiosity was the source of the figurine she had pieced together from the fragments discovered on the bedroom floor. At first she had thought it to be a gag gift of some kind from Ben—since it was obviously a fake or a duplicate. But where would he have gotten it in the first place?

Shauna had never seen the figurine before. *Rameses—Ramsey?* Perhaps it was a subtle joke. But the thing was definitely not authentic, and even if it was, to filch it from the exhibit would get everybody in trouble. It was the sort of thing Shauna would never even consider doing, since she had access on a twenty-four hour basis anyway.

But who would? she thought. Then she thought of the cobra, and of the night of terror, and of the unnerving discoveries that suggested clandestine dangers for people who asked too many questions.

She wanted to know where Ben was, if only to stop fearing for his life.

15

The first thing Slayton was aware of was the heat. It seemed to be very warm, wherever he was.

There was also a low hissing, and sundry noises that his semiconscious mind categorized as "industrial sounds."

Before his closed eyes, the sea of blackness spread out to an imperceptible horizon line. Inky, viscous waves ebbed and flowed according to a rhythm linked directly with the pain. Suddenly, his brain informed him that he was coming up to consciousness, and his pain center added, fatalistically, that he was not going to enjoy waking up very much.

Sounds became sharp and distinct, putting his teeth on edge. A throbbing, persistent ache localized into what felt like a cue ball sutured beneath the skin of his forehead. His back, his arms, were as stiff as basalt, and pulsed with pain. It felt as if his entire back was on fire. Hot.

Ben Slayton opened one eye. Pain seemed to flood in through the opening, eagerly filling remote crannies, causing as much varied agony as possible. His eyes watered up, and he blinked to clear them in the dim, gray light. They ran clean, and he saw indefinite clouds of thin white smoke billowing up to his left. The heat registered again, sharply this time, causing him to clench his teeth and suck air. His eyebrows were brimmed up with sweat, and perspiration trickled in fat beads all over his body. He could feel sweat dripping from his chin. The hissing and clanking became louder, more abrasive.

There was a man with a gun watching Slayton. Slayton

made him out before the man was aware he had come to. Calling in his years of endurance training to fight the pain and the burning sensations, Slayton studied the man through slitted eyes. Sweat drops continued to blur his vision. The thin clouds of wispy smoke seemed to be live steam.

The man was an American, Slayton realized, though not one of the trio he had introduced himself to during the fracas in Shauna's suite. Those men, however, had apparently made their presence felt by pummelling him well after the Rameses VI figurine had conveniently dispatched his consciousness. They were cowards; they worked best with subjects who could not fight back.

He had not yet stopped to wonder how he was maintained in such a position. His legs and knees felt numb. He was being supported—that had something to do with the burning heat presently baking his back and arms. Gravity, however, was doing its best to drag him down to the floor and to sleep. His feet were not touching the floor. Without looking, he angled his toes downward, and by straining for distance, they managed brief contact with the surface below.

Slayton continued to struggle mentally, to keep his restored awareness a secret from the man with the gun as long as possible. He was sitting some fifteen feet away, cocked back in a folding chair, his attention sporadically absorbed by a magazine which he held folded double. Yes, even through the steam Slayton could tell the man was an American. The magazine was in English. The gun was a military-issue Colt .45 automatic, and jutted from a brown leather holster nestled beneath the man's left armpit. He was stripped down to a skintight black T-shirt, and Slayton traced the brown strings of leather holding the shoulder holster in concert with the man's musculature. His coat was draped behind the folding chair.

The hissing was indistinct to Slayton, like the sound of distant hydraulic brakes. He kept his eyes on the man in the distance, and, satisfied that he might get away with turning his head, did so. What he saw looked strange, but gradually assumed proportion and significance in his still-fogged brain.

His right arm—as was his left, he assumed—was lashed straight out from the shoulder to a dull column of silver that seemed to run off to infinity, its wide parallel lines dwindling to a meeting point somewhere in the darkness beyond his field of vision. The lashings ran vertically around the huge pipe—yes, it had to be a big pipe—and held Slayton's arms packed deep within a layer of insulating material. He recognized the lashings as tightly cinched electrical wire—lamp cord. It bit harshly into the flesh of his arms, imprisoning him in a crucifixion posture arranged so that his feet just missed the floor.

His back and shoulders ached dully. He had been hanging for some time—otherwise it would have hurt more. He guessed that he was lashed to a live steam pipe—that explained the heat and the white clouds. And the sweat, and the burning pain. Slayton squeezed his eyes shut, emitting a tiny grunt which the man with the gun did not hear. The ambient noise in the cellar—that's where they had to be, Slayton's mind added, because it was all dingy piping and dust and bricks and noise and darkness—drowned out his small sound of pain.

Slayton tried clenching his fists, bunching the tendons in his arms against the thin bite of the bindings. He could not hope to work them loose, but he could try to pump some blood, and life, back into his arm muscles. Since he was not dead already, he assumed that he would eventually be untied, for some purpose, if only to be killed elsewhere. It would do no good to have arms and legs of stone when they took him down. He had to prepare for any opening in any way he could, and so, discreetly, he wracked his depleted body through subtle isometrics. It would beef up the pain, true, but the pain would keep him from passing out. He made it into an endurance test which was standard procedure for those captured and tortured by the Viet Cong. You made it into a game of pain, and pain thresholds—it was the only way to keep from losing your mind. Some men even grew to need it, becoming addicted to the need to assert themselves against incredible agony. Slayton worked at it, narrowing his concentration down to a thin beam, staring covertly at the man across the room and working up a kind of hate that obliterated much of the superficial pain. He tried to will blood, and life, back into his legs and arms.

Tense and release. Tense and release. Like lifting weights, he thought.

There was no way to gauge passing time, so Slayton ignored it. The important thing was to stay awake.

Chalmers decided to give the man he was guarding some water, in order that he did not fry to death on the steam pipe like a spitted pig. It would do no good to hand over a dead body, not when they needed somebody like Ben Slayton to leave behind after they had finished up their assignment in Washington. A prime scapegoat for assorted mayhem.

He dug an Army canteen out of a canvas rucksack at his feet. It contained plain water. His approach to the bound man on the steam pipe was luxuriously slow.

To Ben Slayton, who watched, it took the man eons just to walk across the room toward him. Perhaps it was a ploy, a subtler form of torture. He had seen the canteen, and having seen it and been allowed to get his hopes up for a drink, the logical thing for the man to do would be to turn and resume his seat, smiling.

"Hey," Chalmers said, patting Slayton on the cheek. His head lolled. "Hey! You still with us, man?"

Slayton cracked his eyes open.

"Here." He tried to tilt the canteen toward Slayton's lips, but had to get closer to do it. There was no danger of his coming loose. Slayton's tongue came out. The water seemed to vanish, be absorbed directly into the tissues without being swallowed. His lips were dry and cracked with white lines.

"Jesus, you're getting a little well-done," said Chalmers. "Can't adjust the heat. Sorry."

Slayton's voice tried to fail him, but he forced it to work. "Who are you?" he managed, in a dry rasp.

A look of pained irritation spread across Chalmers's face. "Come on, man," he said, rolling his eyes. "Don't you guys ever learn? Jesus. Name, rank, and serial shit. Don't be stupid."

"Are you with Haman?" Speaking was painful.

"Man, you've got a hell of an egg on your forehead. I'm surprised your brains didn't fly out your ears. Christ." He tilted Slayton's head up and pressed his thumb into the large purple bruise. Slayton's body stiffened, galvanically. "That hurt?" Chalmers asked, smiling.

"Deke, that pussy bastard," he said. "Probably pounded you while somebody else held you, am I right?"

"Knocked me out," said Slayton.

"Ho, that figures. Deke never could go one-on-one with anybody." He looked up when he saw Slayton's eyes glazing. "Hey man, hey!" He slapped Slayton. "Don't pass out on me, man!"

Slayton's vision stabilized, and he said, "Are you that hard up for conversation?"

"Hey listen," Chalmers said. "We got us a nice long solitary little wait ahead of us. I've read that damned magazine twice and I can't even make a phone call to get a pizza. You wanta know what pain is, buddy? Pain is boredom. Shit!"

There was a constant, background roar in the basement that gave each of Chalmers' words a grating edge, as though his speech blended into the noise to produce a result that could cause physical pain to Slayton's ears. The pauses between his sentences seemed like years.

"Damned thing is, we're gonna turn you loose, man," he said. "See? You're gonna be outta here before you even know it. Just like that." He snapped his fingers. "Later."

Slayton knew full well that could be another hope-and-denial tactic. He chose to ignore it. "Do you always say and do everything in terms of cliches?" he asked, giving up hope of getting any leads in passing from Chalmers' speech.

Chalmers shook his head, almost ruefully. "Wise-ass," he said. "Don't get smart, prick." He dug his thumb savagely into the bruise on Slayton's forehead, the reaction apparently pleasing him. His eyes went a little crazy and unfocused. "I might blow your goddam head off right now."

Slayton was ready for that one. "You can't do anything," he said. "Without orders. You'd squat on the floor and jerk off if Haman ordered you to. You're nothing."

It got the desired response, a stinging slap that rocked his head from side to side against the scorching surface of the pipe. "You're incredibly dumb, man, for a guy who's tied up. You haven't got no brains. You're gonna die if you're not careful!"

Slayton decided to lubricate the man's rage a bit more. He was fairly certain Chalmers was not empowered to kill him. He had to be sure. "I'm tied up and you still can't kill me, you simple-minded dog turd."

That was it. Chalmers drove a fist into Slayton's stomach, and his breath rushed out. And as Chalmers was working on his mad, he failed to see what Slayton could perceive as soon as his eyes refocused. Someone else had entered the basement. A man clad in gray utility clothes, lugging janitorial gear through the door to the security stairway.

"Come on, big man," said Slayton. "Let's see what you're made of besides shit."

Chalmers' eyes flared, and he whipped the gun from the shoulder holster, jacking the hammer back with his thumb. "You talk too much, man," he said, placing the bore of the big gun so it encompassed the tip of Slayton's nose. "You're gonna wind up worm food because you talk too much. Better be nice." He grinned his sickly grin again.

"Fuck you," Slayton said, low and even, calculated for effect. The janitor had spotted them by now, and had moved quietly closer for a better look. He was a man in his mid-thirties, looking somewhat Italian, with a rich mop of curly black hair.

"Dumb," Chalmers said simply. Then he pulled the trigger fast, three times, the barrel of the gun mashed into Slayton's face. He felt the hard clank of the action snapping back, but remained with his eyes steely. To show a man like Chalmers fear was a mistake, even if you were going to die. But Slayton's body tensed against his will, anticipating the bullet that would spread his head and brains all over the basement.

Three dry clicks on a empty chamber. Chalmers saw the fear fleet across Slayton's face. It was a microsecond, but it was enough. He laughed hysterically, high and whooping. He leaned forward, mashing his face against Slayton's, so it appeared as if he had one huge eye in the center of his forehead.

"Big man, big man!" he hooted into Slayton's face. "You're so scared of dying you're making in your pants, big man!" He pulled the clip to the .45 out of his back pocket and waved it in front of Slayton, cackling like a five-year-old who wouldn't share. "You're scared of an empty gun!"

On the words *empty gun*, the janitor broke an industrial

broom handle over Chalmers' skull. His eyes rolled up in his head, and he went down in a pile of unconscious arms and legs, the pistol spinning away on the flat stone surface of the floor.

"Man, what in *hell* is going on down here?" the janitor asked, picking up the gun.

"Treasury agent," Slayton croaked, as though introducing himself. He felt the absurd urge to continue; *treasury agent, janitor; janitor, terrorist.*

The janitor said, "Don't go away," and rushed off for a moment, returning with a pair of wire cutters he used to free Slayton from the pipe.

Agony flared brightly in his arms as they came free. He couldn't help falling in a heap beside Chalmers on the floor when he finally left the pipe. The janitor helped him up. Slayton actually thought he might swoon as blood and fresh pain raced into his depleted extremities.

Slayton pulled himself to his knees. The sensation was at once exhilarating and almost nauseating.

"You have to help me with him," he said, picking up the canteen from where Chalmers had placed it on the floor and drinking—carefully, but greedily. "I'm deputizing you, or employing you, or whatever you want. You'll make a lot of money for a few hours work."

"I hear that," the man said. "This janitorial crap sucks for air. What do I do with this punk?"

"Tie his hands," Slayton said, then adding, "You have a car?"

"Ho, just barely. That's an expensive proposition, and this is the only job a guy like me can get. But yeah."

"What's wrong with you?" Slayton asked.

"You kidding?" said the man. "I came back from Nam to find the employment situation here somewhat—uh, compromised. Now, if I'd been grabbed as a hostage in Iran instead of fighting for Lyndon B. and old Milhous, I might be better off." He snapped off a hank of wire and efficiently immobilized Chalmers, who was still out. "You really a Treasury agent?"

"I'll show you my ID later. After I get some speed into me. What time is it?"

"Eleven o'clock."

"Day or night?" He realized it sounded stupid.

"It's the fourteenth," the man said. "It'll be noon in an hour."

The opening of the Seth-Olet exhibit was in two hours.

16

When Ben Slayton caught his first look at himself in a mirror, he thought he looked like a skid row derelict. And there was no time to get pretty.

The lump on his head was mostly under the hairline, but there was a noticeable bulge that made him look, from the side, like a mutant from a 1950s science fiction movie, and a livid violet crescent that radiated downward onto his forehead. His shirt, from contact with the pipes, had scorched brown along the arms and back. He had numerous cuts and markings from the free-for-all in the suite, and he smelled like the locker room of the Boston Celtics. If he burst in on the Seth-Olet conclave with the wrong timing, he might get himself shot.

He placed an emergency phone call to Winship, who had already gone in with the Secret Service contingent. It stood to reason that everyone else would be in solemn conclave at the exhibit hall. There were phones, but he lacked the numbers, and there was no time left.

Hurriedly, he gave directions to the janitor, his savior, whose name turned out to be Buck Fuller. "Henry, actually," he yelled as they piled into his car, a dusty Camaro Rally Sport. "Buck's from the Marines."

"Move it," yelled Slayton back, feeling the way the bones seemed to grind together as he himself moved. "Break laws!"

The Camaro lept off the pavement, leaving an inch of rubber on the street. They fish-tailed out across an intersection, slewing into the path of a tourist bus and a rank of commuters, but Buck speed-shifted and easily outdistanced them. Slayton braced himself against the padded dash.

"You've done this before," he shouted, smiling. "Faster!"

A wide grin split across Buck's face and he laid his pedal down, screaming through a red light and causing a supermarket tractor-trailer driver to lay on his air horn. The blast dopplered away behind them as they made smoke.

"Thought I was gonna have to take to the sidewalk there for a second!" Buck yelled, eyes nailed to the road, checking his gauges, his mirror, and the openings ahead of him in economical visual sweeps. His hand-eye coordination was uncanny, almost as good as Slayton's.

"There'll be cops on you any second," shouted Slayton. "Can you handle it?"

The grin stayed where it was. "Pie," Buck said.

On cue, a pair of prowlers sprang into view behind them, like cheetahs making tracks behind a gazelle. One slewed in, tires smoking, from a side street, the other screamed into a speed turn, lights and siren bellowing an all-out Code Three. Buck glanced at the mirror, but did not react, saying simply, "They're on us."

"Don't lose them, let 'em follow us in. But don't let them catch up, either."

"Right turn ahead?" Buck shouted.

"Right."

"Watch this!"

With a piercing war whoop, Buck shot the Camaro into the turn, lagging behind on the arc that would slide them into the right-hand lane, and instead spinning the wheel against the line of northbound traffic that loomed in the windshield. With ballsy precision, he rotated the wheel full around in the opposite direction, stabilizing them by spinning the auto completely around in the middle of the street.

They would be simple to follow, thought Slayton: just trace the black lines all over the pavement and find out who was at the end of them.

It was the most exhibitionistic kind of show-off driving, but the cop in the lead chase car could not follow Buck's act. He tried to slow down in order to take the turn Buck negotiated at top speed and spun around anyway, demolishing the front end of a parked Mercedes Benz, clipping his door handles off on a white Dempster Dumpster, and finally shrieking to a stop with a pair of front flats and a copious amount of gray smoke billowing from the wheel wells and under the hood. The second cruiser caught control of its fish-tailing, and blasted past its out-of-commission buddy just as the cop stepped from his wreck to check the damage, pinch himself, and wonder how rich the driver of the Mercedes he had tattooed might be.

"Sorry about that," yelled Buck.

"Idiot's own fault," shouted Slayton back. "He took the driving course but never thought it was for real!"

Parked cars and buildings flashed by in a stroboscopic blur as Buck made time, ignoring the lights. Anyone who could see him coming got hastily out of his way.

"That's it!" he yelled.

"Keep going," Slayton said. "A block and a half there's a turn-in to an alley. Take that. The alley dead-ends. Stop there!"

In the mirror Buck saw the second police car jounce onto the road in their wake, flashbar winking insistently. Then he caught the mouth of the alleyway and careened into it. Though the alley was much narrower than the urban street, Buck did not slow down until they were almost eating the phone poles and chain-link fence that terminated the passage.

"Now what?"

Slayton jacked the door open and stepped out. Behind them the cruiser roared down the alley. "Give yourself up," he said. "Tell them what I told you. I'll have the Secret Service keep them from shooting you. And wait for me!" He slammed the door and ran toward the exhibit hall breezeway.

The grille of the police car filled up the rearview mirror as Buck took his hands off the hot wheel, looked at them, and then folded them in his lap, striving to look as innocent and harmless as possible. "Righto," he said to the mirror.

Two Secret Service men bracketed the entrance to the hall. Slayton ran up and they immediately became defensive.

"Slayton!" he shouted, and luckily one of the men recognized him. He stopped, breathless, and demanded, "Is the President here yet? And is Ham Winship in there?"

"President's due any minute, sir. Winship's inside."

"Then get out of my way," he said, pushing past, and

leaving the men to resent their assigned superiors. No time for ginger treatment of egos, he thought.

Everyone was assembled in the main exhibit room amid the television setups and the artifacts of Seth-Olet's *mastăba*. Several additional Secret Service men sprang to check Slayton as he burst into the room, but fortunately, he spotted Winship before they spotted him.

"Ham!" he shouted. Indecorous, but under the circumstances the best way to get Winship's attention quickly, since he hated the nickname Slayton had come up with for him.

Two more Secret Service men caught up with him as he reached Winship. They started to grab the dishevelled, wild-looking man, but Winship pushed away their eagerness.

Everyone in the room watched the hurried and hushed conversation that followed, like a quick football huddle. To these onlookers, the actions taken in the next few seconds on behalf of the bedraggled man who had burst into the room—where any minute they would be addressed by the President of the United States himself—must have seemed quite odd.

First, the Secret Service men withdrew, with crisp, business-like motions. Winship walked over to the lectern that had been positioned for the television cameras and requested that the room be immediately cleared. Most of the audience complied, thinking this request had something to do with the arrival of the Chief Executive.

But second, and stranger, a member of the elite contingent of archeologists was intercepted as she tried to make her way over to the bedraggled man. She was rather directly escorted out of the room by the pair of Secret Service agents seen talking to the man, led away with gentle but unmistakeable pressure from the men flanking her.

Most of the people in the room took the seeming evacuation in stride.

Shauna Ramsey had come to her feet the moment Slayton rushed in. But the crowd was milling around rather than stationed in their seats, and she had to elbow her way somewhat ungracefully through them. She did not hear Winship's announcement. She could not see anything ahead of her except the mess that had recently been made of Benjamin Slayton. He was alive!

She was halfway to him when her path was obstructed by

a pair of unsmiling Secret Service men. They were wearing gray-on-gray suits, just as Ben had joked during the ride down. They gently grasped her by the biceps and did not permit her to pass.

"Ben?" she said, now confused. *"Ben!"* She shouted at him, across the room, as the agents restrained her, with little show but great efficiency.

He saw her, was looking at her from across the artifact-choked chamber. He saw what was happening to her—and did nothing. He stood there, not taking his eyes off of her, as Shauna Ramsey was conducted away from the room under guard.

Shauna's stomach felt as though it had taken a dive down an elevator shaft. She fought for words but none came.

Something had gone horribly wrong.

"Ben! Jesus Christ, Ben, what the hell is going on?" Slayton turned as Shauna was taken through the door and came face-to-bruise with Wilma Christian. As he turned, she saw the full picture formed by the bashes and cuts, and drew in a small breath of surprise. "Holy god, Slayton, what happened to you?" The diamond-chip blue eyes were irised wide with sudden concern.

"Wilma, you've got to leave," he said, ignoring her, with his eyes past her. Most of the people were already out. Shauna was gone.

"Like hell you say," she snapped instantly. "What are you—" She broke off as Slayton moved around her and began to scan the table areas, searching as rapidly and succinctly as he was capable. His fingers traced mouldings and borders, he weaved and bobbed and gave every object, every surface, every chunk of ancient Egyptian incunabula that came within his reach a thorough once-over. Two more Secret Service men bustled into the room and began doing the same.

She was following him, almost duplicating his movements, looking where he had looked, feeling where he had felt, trying to get a hint by association. None came or presented themselves. It did not take the reporter in her long to get exasperated.

"Ben, what is it? Please, goddamnit, tell me what's going on!" He kept moving, searching frantically, upending ornate pots and sounding the Seth-Olet backdrops for clues or leads.

And as he searched, he finally spoke. It did not slow him down. "There's a bomb in here, Wilma, an explosive device. It could be one of a million configurations. It could be any size, and it could be concealed almost anywhere. It could also go off any second now, so please get your ass out of here! Bricklin!" he shouted at one of the agents. "See Ms. Christian out of here before she gets her ass blown off!"

Wilma went for her camera, like a gunslinger, before Bricklin reached her. Slayton whirled, and for the first time their eyes connected. His were full of desperate steel. "And no pictures, Wilma! Get *out* of here before I toss you through the goddam window! *Out!*" He went back to work.

She waved Bricklin's anxious hands away. "I'm going. Hands off, Ace, unless you want to buck the Constitution."

Wilma complied, and was out the door with the rest. Only Slayton and the two agents remained in the room.

"Goddamnit," he hissed to himself. It was wrong, and he was practically panicking. There was no time to do the obvious, which was to slap the location of his objective out of Shauna Ramsey. Anybody could hold out for an hour. They did not even have *that* much time. The President would not be allowed near the place, but in all probability the roomful of near-priceless artifacts would go up in a brilliant display of fireworks, and Rashid Haman would have another propaganda victory to add to the dossiers.

Which was the real reason Slayton was hanging in the exhibit hall, risking his life on behalf of a tombful of dead antiquity. He had come this far, had been through so much on behalf of Rashid Haman, who up until now had been an incorporeal super-entity, like an omnipotent ghost. To have such an adversary turn out to be a woman who had completely bamboozled him was bad enough—but having her win, despite his realization, in any small way at all, which included the destruction of the exhibit, was a personal defeat that Slayton would rather die than countenance. Losing, at this extreme, would be as bad as death anyway. So Slayton stuck, and searched. The Secret Service men did the same because they were under his orders. It was 12:52 p.m.

"Bricklin! Madison!" he shouted. The men perked up, across the room from him. "Out!" he commanded.

Ten seconds later, Slayton stood alone in the image-perfect recreation of Seth-Olet's final resting place. He spun around, trying vainly to take in everything, realizing he could search for weeks and not cover it all.

His skull was throbbing in pain. The codeine Buck Fuller had given him out of his glove compartment was already beginning to run thin in his bloodstream, and the pain was accumulating again. He slumped against the multiple coffin of Seth-Olet. For all intents and purposes, this was the centerpiece of the collection. The *Ushabtiu* figurines and Canopic jars were arranged as Shauna had described. The truckloads of Seth-Olet's possessions and offerings littered the periphery. And Ben Slayton, knowingly backed into a corner, forced himself to think exactly like one of his worst enemies.

What would Haman do?

He looked up and found himself gazing directly into the dead, blank monster-eye of one of the television cameras. It was angled on the lectern, erected very near the multiple coffins—as out of place in a tomb as you could get.

There would be no time or opportunity to gimmick the camera properly, so that left the lectern.

It was solid wood with carved molding. He tapped it out. Not hollow. Too uncomplicated to conceal anything. He tipped it up and checked the base. Nothing. He set it down with a thump. Then, with his back to it, he turned slowly, scanning the layout of the tomb in reverse from the podium.

The prime object in his line of sight was the coffin, whose foot was angled toward the podium, and thence toward the camera, so that it would dominate the television picture. Slayton moved back to the coffin.

It was actually three boxes, one within the next. The ornate lids were designed to make themselves secure, and proved troublesome for one man working alone. They did not prove impossible to manage, however, and Slayton got the primary box unlidded with little real effort. Quickly he searched the interior, and the space allowed for the subsequent boxes. Nothing.

He made short work of the second lid, and of the third. Nothing came of these searches except a face-to-face with the remains—slightly reconstituted, of course, so they did not disintegrate on contact with air—of Seth-Olet himself. The shriveled, diminutive form grinned blankly up at Slayton, offering neither clues nor aid, suggesting soft death.

Slayton did fast measurements with his hands. He wanted to smash into the coffins with his fists, to yell out *I know it's here, it has to be!* But he forced a chilling composure on himself. His estimates were fast and sure.

Between the second box and the one actually containing the mummy, he came up a palm-width short in depth. He sounded the apparently solid surface beneath his hand. It did not resonate the way the other components of the multiple box sounded when he knocked, and in that instant his heart jumped.

He snatched an ornamental gold dagger from one of the flanking tables, and used it to pry up the veneer, fully aware that he was possibly desecrating Seth-Olet's coffin. "You'll forgive me, old boy," he said to the mummy.

The strip that abruptly peeled up into Slayton's hands had been nailed down with extremely thin, needlelike nails, the betraying holes caulked in and carefully matched with the age and color of the surrounding layers. He wrenched it up and the strip broke free along half the length of the second box.

Under it, nestled in black against a steel backing plate that had been installed in the head of the coffin, was a series of metal pipes, capped with screw-lids at the far end and—Slayton knew—ground down at the near end, the foot end, the end pointed directly at the lectern from behind. The pipes were packed with explosives; the concussive force of the detonation, seeking the path of least resistance, would burst the sanded-down ends of the pipe-bombs, and whatever payload was stuffed into those ends, along with the crude shrapnel produced by the exploding pipes themselves, would blow out through the foot of the coffins with thousands of foot-pounds of explosive pressure.

The resultant blast would not only demolish the President at the appropriate moment, but kill whoever was to his left, destroy a great portion of the tomb-room display, and provide some of the most sensational videotape footage in history, since the camera would be destroyed too—but the last images it would relay to the video trucks outside the exhibit hall would be of pieces of the President, flying directly into the lens. It was at once terrifying and inspired.

There was no telltale aroma of acid, however. Slayton searched and discovered a tiny plastic box wired to the charges, recognizing it immediately. It was a relay junction, connected to a bank of acid batteries, which meant that the lethal weaponry he had discovered was not on any sort of time-delay fuse, as he had feared. It would not go off until it was commanded to—in this case, by flipping a switch on a control-broadcast box very similar to a television remote-control. Or perhaps it was wired up to the cameras.

His heart thudded away freely now. The veins in his neck bulged, flooding pain into his battered head. With a swift and sharp movement, he disconnected the relay box. Now the pipe-bombs could be lifted out with relative safety, and de-activated. Only then did he dare to glance at his watch, and when he did, he felt a quiet wave of indescribable relief wash over him, his forehead breaking out in nervous sweat.

It was 1:02 p.m.

17

Winship involuntarily shut his eyes when his railroad watch—a gold, extremely hardy paternal heirloom and one of his few concessions to personal extravagance—tolled one o'clock straight up. By two minutes after the hour, his metabolism wanted to panic. Quarts of acid released themselves into his stomach. Discreetly, he belched to himself, suffering with the sour taste. It did not a bit of good.

It took eight more interminable, physically draining minutes before Ben Slayton—or, considering his condition, what was left of Ben Slayton—walked out the exhibit hall door and made a beeline for him.

The Presidential motorcade resembled a circle of settlers' wagons, and the Secret Service was everywhere.

"Take them in," Slayton said to Winship. "It's safe to go in. Let's get this damned thing over with."

Winship felt the irrelevant urge to ask Slayton if it was safe. His trust in his agent stopped him.

Another agent approached, and waited for Slayton's attention to turn to him. His question seemed to be one thing, maybe the only thing, Slayton had not thought about. He stopped, looking from the agent to the automobile, Department-issue, from which he had come.

"No," said Slayton at last. "Keep her here, with you, under guard, in that car, until I get back to you."

The agent nodded and returned to the car.

"Do you have to go in there right away?" Slayton asked

Winship. "I have a brief favor to request; it'll take just a minute."

Winship was taken aback. "What?"

"It concerns that rather bewildered-looking police officer standing over there."

Officer Michaels watched the pair approach him. The derelict who had lit out from the speeding Camaro was dragging some government bigwig over to complicate his day. Goddam well told, he thought. He was sick of letting these sons-of-rich-daddies off with a slap on the hand. He wanted to find some hard legal point and make it stick. Michaels was tired of being pushed around. Michaels was hopping mad.

Three minutes later, Michaels told his partner, Officer Craddock, to release the hippie they had collared from the Camaro. He was gritting his teeth as he did it. He was thinking about requesting a transfer to one of the swill-hole districts, so he could take out his aggressions on Puerto Ricans. He was thinking about murdering a bottle of 80-proof, and maybe not waiting until he was off duty to do it.

"Lighten up," said Craddock, once the two men were back in their cruiser. "That kid's a hell of a driver, and nobody got hurt."

The resultant barrage of shouting nearly pushed out the windows of the cruiser as it plowed down the alley, backward, wasting its steel-belted radials all the way.

"Come on," Slayton said to Buck Fuller. "If you'd like to meet the President, now's your chance. You can bitch to him about the situation for vets."

Buck shot back an expression that told Slayton that was the *last* thing he wanted to do.

"Then follow me, and I'll introduce you to the antiquities of jolly old Egypt. Tell me, Buck, does a thousand dollars an hour sound like reasonable compensation for your time and the applications I've made of your singular driving skill?" He did not wait for Buck's reaction before he said, "Good. That fatherly gentleman over there—" He indicated Winship. "—will draw the funds for you later, or I'll know the reason why. Let's go." Slayton's levity was forced. On the way back to the exhibit hall he could not keep from glancing back toward the parked Impala sedan where Shauna Ramsey would be held until he checked in with the agents inside.

Wilma rushed up as they made the door. "Not until after," Slayton said, anticipating her questions. She looked flustered, but said, "I wanted to find out if you'd stopped bleeding yet. I should have known; no blood in *you.* Just a lot of black ink—the kind in government ledgers—and vinegar." Together they entered.

Winship was waiting for the group on the cleared front row of seats. On the opposite side of Camera One was Professor Willis and Maggie Leiber. Willis looked preoccupied as Maggie talked and gestured, apparently prepping him right up to the last minute, despite their witnessing Shauna's removal from the exhibit hall.

Slayton knew he would have to make his excuses to them. They had trusted him. And so—President be damned—he crossed in front of the camera to meet them. But speech-making turned out to be the least important of topics.

"Mr. Rademacher, I trust the area is secure?" Willis said, clinically. It was a sure bet he would not bring up Shauna.

Slayton nodded.

Willis continued. "That's reassuring, I suppose, in light of what just happened. The Arab workers opted not to show for this, and we found out why. We just got the phone call."

"What?" Slayton said in a hoarse whisper.

"That fellow Bassam," said Maggie. "And Ahmed Sadi. They just discovered them in the hospital, both dead. Apparently they . . . they killed each other." Maggie turned her head away. "Oh, damn, the cameras are going to catch something embarrassing, I just know it!"

One of the cameramen turned directly to Willis and said, "They want to know if the visual setup for the podium is the way you want it, sir."

"Who wants to know?" said Willis, distracted.

"The director, sir," he said, tapping his headset. "In the truck."

"Oh. Oh yes, tell them it's just fine."

"No, it's not," said Maggie, biting her lip and considering the area display before them. "Let me think a minute."

"Three minutes," the cameraman said. In the rear of the room the Presidential entourage was causing a good deal of press commotion. It was a session that Wilma did not feel obligated to participate in.

Slayton saw Maggie reappear, holding one of the glittering Canopic jars. "Missing. I knew something was off-balance," she said as she passed the camera and placed the jar at the foot of Seth-Olet's coffin, along with the other three. Slayton had noticed them during his search, but he had not counted them.

"Okay," she said. Everyone was moving in the general direction of assigned seats.

"Maggie," Slayton said. "What the hell was all that about?"

"Oh—I guess it got shuffled out of place while the Secret Service was giving this place the once-over this morning. It's okay now."

Slayton seemed unfocused now. "Ahh—look. After this is all over, I suppose I'll have to explain about—"

She stopped him by taking his face in both her hands, cradling it. "Ben, Ben—don't apologize. You've really done a smashing job. I mean it."

Their eyes locked directly amid the hubbub of news cameramen filming the President's approach toward the lectern, up a narrow aisle between the files of seated guests. Slayton grasped Maggie's hand and turned it against his face, kissing the palm lightly. She let the hand linger. But his eyes did not leave hers. Across the room, Wilma saw the action and bristled. But there was no time to watch that, as the assigned spectacle was about to begin.

Slayton was looking into her eyes still as he spoke, his jaw muscles working: "Goddam it. . . ."

He jumped into motion as though electrified, heading straight for the President at the lectern. A grip was instructing the Chief Executive on the particulars of the microphone. At the sight of Slayton sprinting for them, both men looked up as though offended. On the periphery, the Secret Service agents moved in instantly, and then caught themselves. Winship's eyes were glued to Slayton's moving form.

"Sir! Get down!" was all Slayton yelled as he passed the lectern, shoving the President to the far side and leaping straight for the cluster of Canopic jars, grabbing the one Maggie had placed so carefully.

Straightening, he cast frantically around and saw no outs. Without any hesitation, and with the jar cradled in one arm, Slayton delivered a forearm smash to the photographic backdrop, punching his way through the heavy gypsum board, then jumping through, whirling like a basketball ace going for the perfect lay-up. His back against the wall, he used both arms to hook the Canopic jar through the window over ten feet above his head. His grunt of exertion and the sound of shattering glass came together.

Slayton thought he heard the jar itself break somewhere outside. He never was sure.

The assembled audience came right up out of their seats when the dual explosions blew out the rest of the windows on the east side of the exhibit hall building. Slayton fell to his knees as finely broken glass and fragments of window framing rained down on him from above.

The blast seemed to punch all the air out of the cavernous room, making it impossible to hear anything but a vague roar. But again, to Slayton, there was no time. He moved with as much agility as he could scare up, back through the door he had created for himself in the "side" of Seth-Olet's tomb.

Slayton was finished running. The Secret Service boys had collared Maggie Leiber, alias Rashid Haman, when she tried to dash out the entrance. He stopped, his arms dropping to his sides, his work completed, as the woman glared at him from the door across the chamber, her eyes twin embers of hatred, and her mien that of a cornered badger.

The entire sequence from Maggie's entrance with the bomb had been captured for posterity on camera by the videotape crews. Despite that, Slayton caught sight of Wilma with her camera, snapping everything and looking quite pleased.

Her last shot was of the bristling Maggie, in the grip of the Secret Service.

18

During a varied, if dull, supper, conversation hubbed on whatever needed to be clarified, in ascending order.

Slayton had considered lying to Shauna Ramsey, telling her she had been removed and taken to the Secret Service car for her own protection . . . but that held no water at all when one considered that he had allowed the President to waltz right into bomb range. Long before he walked out of the disorder in the exhibit hall, he had decided to tell her the truth and leave judgment to her.

A sophisticated electronic triggering device had been found in Maggie Leiber's bag, as she was searched. She had known instantly that Slayton had deactivated the directional bombs in the coffin case, and had brought her backup system into play with no delay or fumbling. For Slayton, the key to Rashid Haman lay exclusively in the concept of boxes-within-boxes, or, in her case, backup systems for backup systems. As Haman, she covered each of her plans so well, that by reverse reasoning, one might be able to predict her actions—within limits.

But you never could figure all the angles, he thought.

The long session in Shauna's hotel bathtub—the one to be found in her *third* suite in as many days in Washington—had stripped the layers of the ordeal from Slayton's hide. He felt physically clean and psychically purged. Not only was the spectre of Rashid Haman now resolved into a real person, subject to the laws governing real things as opposed to legends, but the wraith that had bookmarked itself in the back of Slayton's mind as an unsettled score—the ghost of his former buddy, Barney Kaufman—was finally laid to rest.

"I suppose you could never be accused of what we might call sex discrimination when it comes to terrorists," Shauna finally said. "Not only Maggie, but me. We both turned out to be viable."

"Shauna, you couldn't have been set up more professionally," Slayton said. "I overstepped my own specialty. I had the interests of the assignment at heart." He realized that that sounded wrong. "What I mean is—"

"Did you?" she said, searching his eyes for an answer. "I think maybe you lusted to nail Haman too much. You were so crazy to get him—or her—that everybody became a suspect. You lacked faith in me just a little, don't you think?"

"Shauna," he said finally, aware of the handling required. "Listen. I was sure. And I was wrong. If you could see the documentation, the files, you'd realize that it was better to proceed this way, even though it meant trampling a few egos in the process. We came out safe. I won't argue on this score; I think you know the importance of what I'm saying.

"I fell into more than one trap along this investigation. Pegging you was just another defect of my logic. Haman—or Maggie—was never in the habit of leaving a surfeit of clues. I got myself manipulated. And I turned out to be wrong. But we're both still here. What I'm more concerned about than anything right now is whether you think this is all bullshit."

Slayton knew he was prompting a long, meditative silence there in the close bathroom. He sank deeper into the steaming tub. He had nothing more to say if Shauna was determined to hate him for doing his job. Perhaps the worst thing about it was that it would not have been the first time such a judgment had been passed on him.

"Okay," she said. "This time, you've made *your* speech. And whether you blew it or not is largely irrelevant. But I'm going to make one stipulation, here." She was totally serious. "I want to see everything on Rashid Haman, or Maggie Leiber. Everything." Her tone suggested that she already found the task unattractive. "I spent nearly a year living with her, working with her—do you have any idea how hard all this is to accept on a rational level?"

"My point exactly," said Slayton. "The first broad stroke—

in fact, an ideal starting point—for concealing your identity is misdirection. And perhaps the greatest, and therefore the most effective, misdirection is to make the enemy think you're the opposite sex. Saves a lot of trouble when it comes down to the other particulars, which are all artifice anyway. If you could succeed where she succeeded, the frostings on such a misdirection are fairly simple."

He knew he was still speechmaking. Perhaps he needed to get it all off his chest—though he would have hated to admit it in those terms. He broke the silence by adding, "And yes, Shauna, I'll show you everything you want to know. If anyone is entitled, you are."

She touched the lump on his head, gently. "You look like hell," she said.

Slayton said, "No, I'm okay." Whereupon he let his eyes roll up and sank beneath the surface of the water with a gurgle and a theatrical show of bubbles.

"I ought to hold your head under," she said, mostly to the bathroom.

After more frothing, Slayton's mouth surfaced and he said, "I only go down once, not three times, you know, so if you're going to save my ass, don't wait. Glurg!" It left ripples behind when it sank.

"Nut." She nodded her head in sober judgment. And then she climbed into the tub, overflowing it, straddling the surprised Slayton. She was fully clothed.

Arms came out of the water and pulled her down to his waiting mouth.

She had intended to catch a bath before dinner anyhow.

The table consisted of Shauna and Professor Willis, Ben Slayton and Wilma Christian, who managed to keep her mouth shut and be civil to Shauna.

"The pivotal element was the American trainees," said Slayton. "They were all under Maggie's orders, of course, but I attributed stunts to her that were accomplished by them. I didn't consider it until you showed me the pictures taken on the dock, Wilma."

"What 'stunts,' Mr. Rade—I mean, Mr. Slayton?" Willis had long since washed away his shock at Maggie's true identity with his more characteristic curiosity.

"The stunt with the forklift, for example," he replied. "It was pulled off by a man from the very next section of the warehouse, entering and leaving through a door concealed by all the junk. That door—" (which had turned out to be located directly beyond the position of the cart upon which Slayton had leaped to safety) "—was the reason he could get away without being seen. It was also a beautiful implication of the workers in the warehouse, since we never suspected the rooms were linked."

"An intricate sensibility for plans with many layers," Wilma said.

"Like the coffin boxes," said Shauna. "One inside the other."

"Right. If everything had turned into the disaster it was supposed to, later, she knew I'd remember lots of little details and damn myself for not figuring it out sooner. Part of her game—and, of course, one does such things only when one is confident of winning." He punctuated this with a sip of his wine, a passable Rhineskeller.

"Haman implicated Bassam, whose only value was being an available victim," Shauna said. "As soon as he got actually involved—by handling the cobra and planting it, under her orders—he was useless as a diversion. So she eliminated him in a manner designed to cause the most confusion and get the most things done in one fell swoop: she primed him, with threats of revealing his identity and her leverage as Haman, and then pointed him at Ben. His coming after Ben provided a new scapegoat—namely me, since I was the one who suggested he consult Maggie on the Arab work crew in the first place."

"And when I suspected Shauna," said Slayton, "the first person I tried to probe was Maggie. Direction was easy after that. A plant in Shauna's room—if I had *really* had it together about Egyptology, Professor, I would have known the statuette was a phony, and that would have discounted Shauna. But I didn't think. Everything on the tour, every artifact, had to be accounted for, which meant anything that expendable had to be fake. And since you found the fourth Canopic jar, we have to assume the one I tossed out the window was fake, too. I'm afraid that despite all this violence, Egypt's heritage is intact—and not much good as a propaganda victory."

Wilma snickered, across the table.

"The other connection I missed was even more obvious. And it shows a conflict of intention as well, but perhaps only in retrospect."

"A bomb was planted in Ben's car immediately after Maggie sought him out and spoke to him directly for the first time. She sounded him out. And the attack in the hotel suite followed another consultation. Ben's nosing about upset her enough to react immediately. " Shauna paused. Wilma was still covering a smile with her napkin.

"Okay, out with it," said Slayton.

"It's not relevant," she said. "It's the Chevy."

"Oh, god, yes. Two explosions. When I heaved the Canopic jar out the window, it smashed through the front window of a parked car and blew the car up. It belonged to Groth—the Sparta security guard."

"The one who was abusing everybody?" said Willis, and Slayton nodded. This time the laughter rang around the table.

"Talk about a grand slam, though," said Wilma. "When I think about that bomb setup, Ben, I think you're right. How arrogant and ostentatious could you get? That's a mind that knows the true value of media."

There was a renewed silence, which Slayton finally broke by saying, "Now, Wilma, about your story . . ."

"Hold it!" she said. "Exclusive rights, remember? Unemcumbered access to details. I've already talked this over with Mr. Winship." She lagged for the benefit of the punchline. "You're just going to have to have faith, Ben, because right now your life is in the hands of the fourth estate."

Slayton groaned.

". . . which needs some TLC from me at the moment if I'm to meet my deadline. We all have our bosses; mine happens to be a clock tonight. I hate to do this, but you guys will have to get along without me—I've got to go." She was looking at Ben directly, and she knew what she was saying. The friendly argument was due for another time.

"Don't forget," she added, nailing Slayton. "Coat of Arms. Your treat." With that, she was gone. Slayton watched her leave, thankful for the escape hatch she had smoothly offered him.

"I'm afraid I must opt out soon, myself," said Willis.

"Without—you know—there's that much more to be done and the schedule has not gotten any lighter for us." He seemed to be dealing pragmatically with the whole circumstance. "And as Ms. Christian has graciously offered to drop me at the hotel, and since she in all probability does not want to wait forever for me out front, I suppose I should bid you both good night and thank you, sir, for the excellent dinner. Although I think the name Rademacher suits you, young man, gross fabrication or no."

"More German and disciplined, perhaps?" suggested Shauna. Willis seemed to consider it as he left.

Once again the two were alone and in silence.

"Ben, tell me something else. That thing with Bassam, the Arab worker, and poor Ahmed—" she trailed off.

"Bassam," he said. "Poor little son of a bitch. He was running scared all the way, and the damned irony of it is that he left Egypt to get away from the terrorism there." He seemed to take a tangent of his own. "It'll be that way everywhere, if someone doesn't crack down."

The anger started to boil up again when he considered the boisterous, lively Ahmed, killed in his own hospital room by the same sorts that attacked him in the suite. Everyone was under orders. The protection the police provided in the hospital was not as dependable as that afforded by the Sparta men. Then he said, "That's not really what's bothering you."

"I want to know what's going to happen to—"

"You want the flowery version, or you want the truth?"

She said nothing, meeting his gaze levelly.

"Alright. She's probably arranged for the local contingent to attempt to spring her within a specified time. But we wanted her too badly for us to fool around now that we've got her. Her location will be a secret. There's probably ten fake leads an hour coming directly from Winship's office. She's an international criminal. So many different agencies want her that dividing her up will be the hardest part. And there will be a long time—mentally long—in which she will realize her cavalry isn't going to show, after which she will do her best to kill herself."

"Oh." Her voice had become small and clipped.

"That's it," he continued. "Shauna, when I was thinking of her in terms of Haman the terrorist, I wanted to break her neck myself. Bare hands. But in the exhibit hall, just for a second, I was able to see past her eyes, directly into her soul, like a flash of lightning. She's locked into the life she chose years ago, and she knew it was a life that offered no recriminations and no compromises if things were to go wrong. Entropy pulls you along after enough time. She could never be anything else; it permeated her life the way the smell of fluoric acid and plastique stayed on her hands when I caught a whiff of it."

"The smell clued you in?"

"Together with her eyes, yes. And after that second, I didn't want to kill her, I just wanted her neutralized—and now she'll neutralize herself, in a matter of days . . . and don't shake your head at me, because I know whereof I speak. I'd do the same thing, and we're not unalike. It's true. I don't wish to forget it since there's too much to be learned. But I would like to stop thinking about it for a while."

"Me too," she said, making a helpless sort of shrug. "It will take a lot of time, though. You're right . . . she wasn't exactly a bosom friend, but I—"

"I know," Slayton said, closing the topic.

"Remember the nine components of man? The Egyptian parts?" she said. "Somehow I seemed to divine that that last part, the *ren,* wasn't right with you. Your name." She sipped. "And you missed your chance to find out about the other parts. Forgive me a question, Ben, but why are you even alive now?"

"Scapegoat," he said, recalling the intimations of Chalmers, in the basement dungeon of a faceless apartment complex somewhere across town. "The whole setup was very obviously designed to make me look negligent as hell: dead President, destroyed exhibit, film at ten. I owe the nonrealization of that rather bleak scenario to a fellow nobody knows, named Buck Fuller. Henry Fuller. Vietnam vet, just like myself, and probably just like some of Haman's sinister trainees. There are guys like Chalmers, who are responsible for a lot of the strife in this country . . . and then there are guys like Buck Fuller.

"And as for my pseudonym, my apologies to you and the Professor," he added, lightening. "I quite like Rademacher, the more I think of it. I may use it again someday."

"When you check into a hotel with a strange woman?"
"Not a strange woman. An enigmatic one."

Her eyes were downcast. "The *tour* part of the tour commences next week. A couple of months from now it all winds up, in Los Angeles. And that'll be it." She ran her finger contemplatively around the lip of her own wineglass. "I have no idea what my life will become after that. The tour is the resolution of the whole thing that began with Willis' discovery of the tomb, the *dénouement*. Scientifically, after that, it's all repetition.

"But right here, right now," she said, abruptly, "you and I have a night, and beyond that, a week. And beyond that, in the future somewhere, I suspect we may have a few more."

Like the dancer in the long-ago Tangier cabaret, her eyes now pooled darkly and invitingly. "And I'm satisfied with that. Those in the domain of the gods paid particular attention to the times of twilight, and dawn, and dusk. The divisions and distinctions between darks and lights were finely drawn. The folks in charge now are Nephthys, the evening, and Set, the night. Here, this is for you."

She came up from her bag with a small charm of solid 24-karat gold. "It's an *ankh*, a life symbol. The corniest Egyptian thing I could think of."

Ben Slayton very often had to graph his life in terms of violence and respite. Now it was life's turn. He accepted the little *ankh*. "I take it this is not from Seth-Olet's inventory," he said, turning it over and over, pleased with the gift.

"Actually it's from a local department store," she said. "In America, they're practically pop. Like pyramids. And now, I want to go for a long, slow walk in the cold."

"And check into a hotel using a phony name?" He clasped the *ankh* tightly in his hand.

"Something like that." She smiled.

After a traumatic week, Slayton and Shauna were battered and disillusioned, yet very much alive. Slayton kept the *ankh* in his grip, as they walked out into the chill Washington night.

MYSTERY...SUSPENSE...ESPIONAGE...

THE GOLD CREW
by Thomas N. Scortia
& Frank M. Robinson *(B83-522, $2.95)*
The most dangerous test the world has ever known is now taking place aboard the mammoth nuclear sub *Alaska*. Human beings, unpredictable in moments of crisis, are being put under the ultimate stress. On patrol, out of contact with the outside world, the crew is deliberately being led to believe that the U.S.S.R. has attacked the U.S.A. Will the crew follow standing orders and fire the *Alaska*'s missiles in retaliation? Now the fate of the world depends on what's going on in the minds of the men of THE GOLD CREW.

DOORS
by Ed McBain *(B91-937, $2.50)*
Meet Alex Hardy. He can plan and execute a robbery with consummate skill. He can seduce a woman with equal skill. But now he is faced with the most beautiful woman and the most difficult job he has ever encountered. Bone-chilling tension.

THE FRENCH ATLANTIC AFFAIR
by Ernest Lehman *(B95-258, $2.75)*
The S.S. Marseille is taken over in mid-ocean. The conspirators are unidentifiable among the 2,000 other passengers aboard. Unless a ransom of 35 million dollars in gold is paid within 48 hours, the ship and the passengers will be blown skyhigh. A first-class ticket to excitement.

YESTERDAY'S SPY
by Len Deighton *(B31-014, $2.50)*
Two friends who spied together. But that was in another time and another place—now they fight on different sides. A spellbinding tale of deceit and terror in a world where political reality destroys the most hallowed allegiances.

RECOVERY
by Steven L. Thompson *(B93-482, $2.95)*
The year is 1982. Max Moss—a daring ex-racer on a specialized American rescue team—is perfect for the death-defying chase in a superspeed car for the recovery of a secret U.S. plane forced down in East Germany by Russian fighter pilots. Everyone is against Max and his partner as they use their wiliest resources to bring the plane's super-secret, biocybernetic device back to safety.

MEN OF ACTION BOOKS

DIRTY HARRY

By Dane Hartman

He's "Dirty Harry" Callahan—tough, unorthodox, no-nonsense plainclothesman extraordinaire of the San Francisco Police Department. . . Inspector #71 assigned to the bruising, thankless homicide detail . . . A consummate crimebuster nothing can stop—not even the law! Explosive mysteries involving racketeers, murderers, extortioners, pushers, and skyjackers; savage, bizarre murders, accomplished with such cunning and expertise that the frustrated S.F.P.D. finds itself without a single clue; hair-raising action and violence as Dirty Harry arrives on the scene, armed with nothing but a Smith & Wesson .44 and a bag of dirty tricks; unbearable suspense and hairy chase sequences as Dirty Harry sleuths to unmask the villain and solve the mystery. Dirty Harry—when the chips are down, he's the most low-down cop on the case.

#1 DUEL FOR CANNONS *(C90-793, $1.95)*
#2 DEATH ON THE DOCKS *(C90-792, $1.95)*
#3 THE LONG DEATH *(C90-848, $1.95—Coming in December)*